Super Penguin 2

Rob Witzel

Illustrations By Katie Weston

T0284601

SuperPenguin
Publishing Co.

Published by Super Penguin Books LLC

This book should never be used as a flotation device and is harmful if swallowed or ingested...seriously, are you still reading this part? This is the boring stuff, turn a few pages and start there.

Visit our website and social media for more Super Penguin content!
SuperPenguinBook.com
facebook.com/SuperPenguinBook
instagram.com/super_penguin_book

ISBN: 979-8-9903139-0-3

For Parker

Dear Reader,

Thanks for picking up *Super Penguin 2*! I presume if you're reading this, you read *Super Penguin* and can't wait to figure out where Paul Frost's story goes next! If you haven't read the first book, then what the heck are you doing? Who the heck starts with book two? You missed the origin story of the hero! You missed how a seemingly ordinary penguin, working as a sportswriter, got tangled into a major crime operation. You missed how his polar bear friend, Annie, along with the former chief of police, Sam, a lion, teamed up to take down the evil DragonCorp led by the even more evil General Talon, a Komodo dragon. You missed how Talon's right-hand Lyla, a tiger, was captured, and how his top mad scientist Dr. Pigg (a pig, obviously) is still on the loose. Last but not least, you missed Super Penguin learning he has SUPERPOWERS! Should I have started all that with a *"spoiler alert"*? I mean you did pick up a book with "2" in the title and didn't think twice about reading it before reading the first book...but I digress. If you *did* read the first book, then you're well aware that when we last saw our favorite crime fighting penguin, he took down General Talon with an unknown power that emitted from his body. He thought nobody saw him, but *someone* did and left a note in his desk. With all of those cliff hangers, plus DragonCorp being burglarized and the remaining robots now gone...we've got a lot to catching up to do. Let's dive back into the story!
-Rob

Paul sat in the front passenger seat while Annie drove her van to the crime scene.

"You alright?" the polar bear inquired.

"Yeah...I'm fine. I just...never mind we'll talk about it later. Where's Sam? Is he in the loop about the break in?"

"I haven't spoken to him yet. Why don't you give him a call?"

The penguin pulled his cell phone out of his jacket pocket and called his friend.

Sam answered midway through the first ring, "Hey, Paul. Are you guys headed to DragonCorp?"

"Yeah, we are on our way. You're on speaker phone with Annie next to me. Got anything new to tell us?"

"As a matter of fact, I just got off the phone with Deputy Boone. Here's the situation. Chief Yu asked Henry to escort the two of them through the building as someone who would know his way around. Henry took them to the test room where the robots should have been, and he noticed they were all gone. He's taking them to the security office now to check the camera footage."

"Okay, do you still need us to come over there?" Annie chimed in.

"Yeah, I think it would be good to have you here. We can discuss anything we see on the cameras and put a plan together for what's next."

"Sounds good," the polar bear replied. "We'll see you soon."

Paul tapped his phone to end the call. "It's gotta be that Dr. Pigg that was working for Talon. He tried to kill Henry, then me. He created those death machines, so I know he wants them back."

"You're probably right, and who knows what he's planning" Annie said as she continued driving towards the crime scene. "Are you sure you're okay, Paul? I've barely seen you since everything happened downtown, and you've been unusually... distant. Last time I saw you like this was after your parents..."

Paul angrily cut her off. "Annie, I'm fine. I don't want to talk about it." The remainder of the car ride was awkwardly silent.

Though he was no longer talking to his friend, Paul began to think to himself.

"Really? That's how you treat your best friend? She's worried about you, bozo. Just tell her. It's weird, but she'll understand. Won't she? I don't understand it. My whole body glowed purple. And then that purple...whatever it was travelled through me and out of my staff. If I didn't know any better, I'd think it was all a dream. Seriously, though, you should start talking to her again."

Paul opened his beak, but before any words could come out, Annie said, "We're here," as she put the van in park. The penguin began to get out of the vehicle when Annie shouted, "Wait! You need to be Super Penguin, right now. You can't go out there like this." The penguin chuckled with an embarrassed smile. "Good call. I'm still getting used to this *secret identity* thing."

Annie got out of the vehicle while Paul struggled to climb over the arm rests and center console to get to the back of the van. He stumbled a bit but eventually conquered the obstacles and began to change into his uniform.

Directly in front of Annie was the entrance to Dragon Corp. Steps away was where Sam had picked up her, Henry and Super Penguin days before during Super Penguin's escape. Now, there were three police cars parked perpendicularly to the entrance of the facility. The glass doors had yellow police tape strung between the handles. Standing guard was Deputy Boone, the dog who was one of the few who knew Super Penguin's identity. "Good afternoon, Miss Freese," Boone said as he nodded. "Was that Super Penguin I saw somersaulting into the back seat?"

"Yeah, he should be out in a minute."

The bear and the police dog waited while the bird changed. A few moments later, the back doors of the van opened, and Super Penguin emerged from his changing room. He stepped out of the van, but his cape was tangled in one of the seatbelts. As he exited, he was thrown off course and tumbled onto the pavement. Annie and Boone oohed and grimaced in unison. Super Penguin sprang to his feet, dusted himself off, and walked towards his friends.

"We really need to work on your entrances," Annie chuckled as her friend grew closer.

"Remind me to fire whoever put this cape ...oh wait it was you!" He glared at Annie and chuckled. "Alright, so what's the situation?"

"Chief Yu and Chief Hart are in the security office looking at cameras. I'm out here waiting on you two. We think the perps are still inside." Boone pulled out his walkie talkie and hailed the chiefs. "Alright, Super Penguin and Annie are here; do you want us to come to you?"

Sam's voice soon came back on the walkie talkie. "Negative, Boone. We've located the trespassers. It looks like there's a group of four in Pigg's office. All smaller creatures; the biggest one's a fox, and he's with a raccoon, opossum, and skunk. All are in matching black outfits and ski masks. There's also a cheetah in another office. If I didn't know any better, I'd say it's that Michael Myles guy from the hockey team. It looks just like him, but why in the world would he be here? Henry is on his way to help you three. Chief Yu and I will head toward the cheetah. Pa...I mean, Super Penguin, do you remember how to get there?"

"Yeah, I think so," the penguin replied. Boone, Annie, and Super Penguin swiftly walked through the long hallways. At each intersection, Paul scanned their surroundings and made his best guess as to which way to go.

"Are you sure you know where you're going, kid?" Boone asked after the third turn.

"I think so...hey look there's Henry!" The three quick-stepped their way towards the hyena.

"Hey guys, glad to see ya made it. Dr. Pigg's office is just up there." Henry pointed toward the door. The team crept towards the door. They were within about ten paces when the doors suddenly swung open, and the fox, skunk, opossum, and raccoon waltzed out of the office. Each one carried a box of various gadgets, both complete and partially assembled.

"FREEZE!" Boone yelled as he drew his pistol and pointed it at the trespassers.

When Boone yelled, two things happened simultaneously. First, the opossum quite literally obeyed the demand as his entire body went stiff, and he collapsed to the ground. The contents of his box spilled out onto the floor. The second event was not so pleasant for the heroes. The skunk reached into his box and dropped a small, silver orb onto the ground. When it hit the ground, the orb burst open and released a thick, green smoke that quickly filled the hallway. Super Penguin and his friends could not see a thing. They began to cough and covered their mouths and noses. It didn't take long for the smoke to disperse, but when it did, only the incapacitated opossum and his box of gizmos remained. The other three trespassers had escaped.

Boone holstered his weapon and grabbed the walkie talkie. "Sam, it's Boone. We've got one of them, but the other three escaped. They are carrying some kind of smoke bombs and other gadgets, so be careful."

Sam responded in a hushed voice slightly louder than a whisper, "Good work getting the one. Maybe he'll lead us to the others. We are getting close to the office the cheetah was...UGH!"

Sam's voice suddenly stopped and then picked back up. "I don't know what the heck that was…I saw this weird blur coming towards me fifty yards away, and then, like a second later, it collided with me and knocked me off my feet. I…I think it was the cheetah…I know they are fast, but that was incredible. I've never seen anything move that fast…"

"You okay?" Boone inquired.

"Yeah, we're fine. Let's get out of here. We'll meet you out front."

***

The group reunited in front of DragonCorp. Super Penguin noticed his friend, Sam, was limping more than normal. "You okay, boss?"

"Yeah, I'm fine…" the lion dusted himself off for the umpteenth time. Then, he directed his attention to Annie who was carrying the captured opossum. "At least we caught one of them. He's still breathing, right?"

"He's breathing but still not moving."

Boone spoke up, "It's an opossum thing. They play dead when they're scared. He'll probably be like this for a while. Annie let's put him in the back of my car. Let me cuff him first." With that, Annie and Boone walked away from the others.

"Henry, do you have any idea who these animals are?" Super Penguin inquired.

"I think so. I've never met them though, only heard about 'em. There is a group that call themselves the 'Garbage Gang'. Bottom feeders mostly, and pretty low on the crime world ladder. When some of the DC guys would go out and do jobs for Talon, these Garbage Gang goofs would try to sneak in with them and scoop up the leftovers. I imagine they heard this place was vacant and wanted to see what they could steal."

"How about the other guy?" Super Penguin asked.

"From what I saw on the camera, it looked like Myles."

Super Penguin began to think out loud with his peers listening. "I guess that makes sense. He just got banned for life by the hockey league for point shaving for Talon...maybe he's turned to a life of crime?"

Chief Yu spoke up, "It's at least a good starting point for the investigation. I'll send some of my detectives to his house to talk to him. We should probably end your involvement until after you're sworn in."

"Sworn in?" Sam questioned.

"You didn't tell him, Super Penguin?" Yu asked.

Super Penguin awkwardly scratched the back of his head and then answered, "Well...there just wasn't a good time, and I didn't know what you'd say, so I was putting it off, but I was going to tell you."

"Are you guys talking about Super Penguin working for the police?" Annie inquired after she finished her task and rejoined the group.

"What?" Sam bellowed. "Chief Yu, he's not an officer. And Pa..I mean Super Penguin, you haven't gone to the academy or received any formal training. Why am I just now hearing about this?"

Yu replied. "Super Penguin, the interim mayor and I only met yesterday about it. He's not becoming an officer. You guys will continue operating the way you have, as a special taskforce division of the department. It's the only way to keep Super Penguin legal and not labeled as a 'vigilante'. You, Annie, and Super Penguin will all be paid through the department making everything completely legal. We just need to sign a few papers, and then we're having a ceremony to let the public know that Super Penguin is an *official* defender of the city."

"That..." Sam hesitated, now at a loss for words, "that actually sounds really smart. I...uh...good work, Yu."

"I learned from the best, sir," she said as she winked at Sam. "We'll talk later, but I need to get back to work, and again, the *taskforce* needs to leave."

Super Penguin, Annie and Sam filed into Annie's van and drove back home.

***

I know where your power comes from. If you are interested, meet me where it happened tonight at midnight.

Paul laid on his couch holding the note in the air above his head. He'd been wondering about what happened for a week. His body had glowed purple, and he had no answers...but someone did. Who was it? He didn't remember seeing anyone around- just Sam who had passed out, Talon and him, right? Was this a trap? Talon was in jail with no option for bail, so it wasn't him, but it could be one of his goons. Maybe it was Dr. Pigg setting the trap to avenge his boss and finish what he started in the lab. Paul sat like this for hours pondering each possible scenario. Paul's inner monologue was interrupted by a loud KNOCK KNOCK KNOCK on the front door. "Paul? Are you in there?"

"Yeah, just a second," Paul rolled off the couch and tucked the note into his pocket. He made his way to the door, turned the lock, and when he opened the door, he was met by his friend who was holding a warm pie. Paul smiled a tired smile, "Hey Annie, come on in."

The polar bear walked through the doorway. "I just wanted to stop by and check in on you. Plus," she gestured at the dish she was holding as she smiled, "I made your favorite, fish pie. I used your mom's recipe!"

Paul smiled at his friend's kindness. "Thanks, Annie. I'm sorry about earlier today. I'm stressed about 100 other things, and I took it out on you. I just feel like I have this incredible weight on my shoulders, and I'm starting to reach my breaking point. I don't know what to do."

"I know. This hero stuff is pretty intense, and that's actually something I wanted to talk to you about...I was going to bring it up in the van, but...well, anyway. Here, look at this!" Annie pulled out her phone and showed the screen to her friend.

Paul gazed at the image. It was a design for a hero's uniform: a full bear-sized bodysuit. It was dark blue with what looked like a big, icy-blue iceberg that started at the chest and went down to the waist. In the middle of the iceberg was an emerald green T. "Annie, I don't understand...that looks way too big for me...and what does the 'T' stand for?"

"No, silly. This isn't a uniform for you! It's for me! I thought I could be your side kick...I mean... if that's okay with you... I just figured you could use some help out there and someone to share this secret identity life with...I've done most of the same training with Sam that you did, and I even came up with a name...*Tundra*. What do you think?" She looked at the penguin nervously.

Paul started with a little anger in his voice. "Absolutely not, Annie! That's ridiculous!"

Annie's face began to droop into a frown. "But..."

"Let me finish, Annie." Paul interrupted and began to smirk. "You're absolutely not going to be my sidekick. For as long as I can remember, you've been by my side. From elementary school to high school, to college, and at the *Inquirer,* we've always been equals. If we are going to do this together, we are going to be equals in this too. Super Penguin would be happy to work with Tundra, but only under the condition that she is my *partner*. None of this *sidekick* business."

Annie rushed towards Paul and gave him a big bear hug, lifting him off the ground and squeezing. "Oh, thank you, thank you, thank you!"

"Alright, alright, you're going to snap me in half if you squeeze any harder!"

Annie set her friend back on the ground. "Sorry, I'm just really excited."

"It's okay...while we're talking about hero stuff, something happened the other day." Paul paused, still unsure if he should say something about his purple glow and mysterious power.

"Yeah, what is it?"

"Well...um..." Paul suddenly changed course. "Well...I... uh...was wondering if you could shorten my cape a little. It got caught when I tried to get out of the van. Maybe take it up an inch or so?"
Annie laughed. "That happened today, Paul! How hard did you hit your head? Of course, I'll hem the bottom. Was that it?"

"Yeah," Paul lied, "that's it."

"Okay, well, I'm starving. Let's cut into this fish pie while it's still warm." And the two friends began to eat their first meal as official hero partners.

* * *

Paul skipped the meeting with the mysterious note writer and went to bed. When he woke up the next morning, he was a little bit surprised that nothing happened because of his absence. No second note slid through the mail slot. No stranger knocked at his door in the middle of the night. If it was a trap, he had successfully avoided it. But what if the letter came from a fellow do-gooder? Paul was willing to err on the side of caution.

The penguin rolled out of bed, tossed his royal blue robe over his shoulders and while he put his flippers through the arm holes, he slipped on his matching slippers. Paul went to the kitchen, poured himself a bowl of his favorite Yummy-O's cereal, and sat at his kitchen table to enjoy his breakfast. After a few bites, his phone, which was still on his bedroom nightstand, began to ring. Paul quickly scooped two more spoonfuls of cereal into his beak and shuffled back into his bedroom. The caller ID showed it was Boone. Paul answered, "Hello?"

"Good morning, Super Penguin. This is Deputy Boone. We know your taskforce isn't official yet, but the opossum finally snapped out of his frozen state, and we thought you'd want to be here for the interview. Can you be here in an hour?"

"Uh, yeah, I should be able to do that."

"Chief Yu, Chief Hart and Annie will be here too. We'll see you soon."

Paul went back to the kitchen, took the spoon out of his bowl, and poured the remainder of his cereal and milk into his beak. He wiped the milk residue off of his upper beak and then went to put on his Super Penguin gear. He brushed his beak, combed his hair, and packed his tools (just in case). Super Penguin opened his apartment door and was greeted by his neighbor, Gary, a gazelle, who was just returning from his morning run. Gary's mouth dropped open with shock, and it was a few seconds before he spoke. When he did, it was with as much excitement as the mammal could let out "Oh. My. Goodness. Paul...you...you...you have made the absolute *best* Super Penguin cosplay I have *ever* seen. That's so good!"

"Uh...thanks!" The penguin breathed a sigh of relief, smiled, and quickly turned to lock his door. He turned towards the exit and muttered to himself, "Don't figure it out, don't figure it out."

"Wait a minute!" Gary exclaimed with as much energy as he started. Paul began to panic, but thankfully Gary could not see his face. It was tense and scared, his eyes had never been wider, and he was nearly as frozen as the opossum he'd seen the day before. He was sure his annoying neighbor Gary had just figured out his secret identity. "Paul, you silly bird, Comic Con isn't until next weekend!"

The penguin turned back around with a relieved smile. "Haha! Oh, you're right, Gary. Silly me! Well, I'm uh...late for an appointment, so I'd better get going!" Super Penguin didn't wait for a response and hastily walked to the door.

Gary reached for his keys in his jacket pocket and muttered to himself, "Man, that guy is clueless to the world around him, ha! Thought Comic Con was this weekend! What a dingus!"

***

Super Penguin was the last to arrive at the police station. Boone met him at the entrance. "Hey Super Penguin, thanks for being here." The two shook paws and flippers as Boone continued to give a rundown of what was to come. "Annie...uh I mean... Tundra and Chief Hart are already here. You three will be behind a two-way mirror while Chief Yu conducts the interrogation. You'll be able to see them, but they won't be able to see you. You do not need to participate. We just thought it would be helpful for you three to get first-hand information from anything he shares."

"Sounds good," Super Penguin affirmed. Boone led the way. When they got to their meeting place, Super Penguin saw Annie in her Tundra uniform, walked up to her, and held out his flipper for a handshake. "Hello, *Tundra!* It's nice to officially meet my new partner."

Tundra responded with a big smile, "Nice to meet

you too, Super Penguin! I'm very excited to work with you!"

Sam watched with a confused grimace plastered on his face. "You two are weird. Can we get this started?"

A few moments later, after the exchanging of pleasantries, two guards- an elephant and a bull- brought in the opossum who was now wearing an orange jumpsuit and a pair of handcuffs on his wrists. When the opossum sat down in the wooden chair, the guards secured the handcuffs to the table. A few minutes later, a sharply dressed weasel was led into the room by the guards. This was the same lawyer Paul had previously met in Mr. Trunk's office at the *Eagle City Inquirer*, Mr. Zuckerkorn. The weasel sat next to his client, and a few moments later Chief Yu entered with a notepad and pencil. Yu introduced herself to Zuckerkorn, reminded the opossum of his rights, and began the interview.

"I want to remind you both that everything said here today is being recorded and can be used as evidence if and when this case goes to trial. First, please state your name, sir."

"Oliver."

"What's your last name, Oliver?" the lamb patiently asked.

"I... uh...I don't have a last name, ma'am."

"What do you mean you don't have a last name?"

"I never had one because Arthur never gave us one, I guess."

"And who is Arthur?"

"He's the leader of our group. He found every one of us. Some of us were older than others when we were found, but Arthur gave us a place to stay and food to eat. I was just a baby when he found me. He said he saw me in a basket outside the fire station. He said I was screaming and hollering, and nobody else was around to take care of me, so he did."

"Wow...I...I didn't know all that. That's a very touching story..."

"I'm not trying to make excuses or nothin'. That's just how it is and why we take some of the jobs we do."

"By 'we' you mean the group known as *The Garbage Gang*, correct? Is that what you call yourselves?"

"Yeah, I never really liked the name, and I never really wanted to steal. It's just what we have to do to get by it seems."

"What can you tell me about what you were doing at DragonCorp?"

"We were hired to steal some tech. This pig scientist wanted some of his old gadgets and didn't want to be seen, so he hired us to go retrieve them. I was with Frank when he had the meeting, but I wasn't in the meeting, so I don't know a lot about it. All I know is that he wanted us to steal the tech and then use it to break into the prison and bust out his friend."

Startled, Yu demanded clarification, "Excuse me? Did you say *break into* prison?"

"Uh oh, I figured it had already happened while I was out..."

"When were you supposed to do that?"

"What day is it?"

"It's Friday the 12th, about 10am."

"Then the break in is gonna happen right about now."

***

Super Penguin and his peers had heard the entire conversation. Without saying a word to one another, the penguin, polar bear, and lion made their way to the exit and filed into Tundra's van. Yu, Boone, and a team of four more officers led the way in a caravan of three squad cars. The polar bear followed their lead.

The ride started off silent and focused until Super Penguin broke the silence with a quizzical remark from the back seat, "Do you think we'll get a flashing light once we're officially on the taskforce?"

The bear chuckled at her friend, "Really, Supes? We're minutes away from charging into a prison, mid-breakout, and that's the top thing on your mind?"

"I mean...I wouldn't say it's the *top* thing on my mind. It just sort of popped into my head is all."

"Stay focused you two," Sam chimed in, "and we'll *definitely* have flashing lights."

"You don't know that!" bellowed Annie. "We don't have any of the details."

Sam smiled, "Don't need details. We're not doing *any* taskforce *unless* we get the flashing lights. Hey, I just got a text from Boone. They are going to the northeast entrance of the prison, and he wants us to go to the southwest gate. Turn here."

Super Penguin laughed, "I one hundred percent agree. I'm not joining *any* new team without flashing lights. Looks like we're here. Nice driving, Annie!"

"Thanks, but I'm in uniform. It's *Tundra*, remember?"

"Sorry! I'm still getting used to that, *Tundra*!"

"It's fine. So...what's the plan?"

Sam answered first, "Well, for starters, we don't even know if the opossum was telling the truth, so let's gather our facts and..."

As they stopped at the guardhouse, Tundra looked inside the booth and immediately interrupted the conversation. On the ground, they saw an incapacitated buffalo in a security guard uniform. "The guard is down!" Annie exclaimed. She shifted the car to park and quickly exited to aid the downed guard. It only took a moment to notice the red, feathered dart protruding from the buffalo's large neck. "Tranquilizer," she said as she checked for a pulse. "He's breathing."

Sam ordered, "Leave him be. We need to keep going!"

Tundra stood up and pushed a large green button on the control panel labeled GATE OPEN. Once pressed, a pully mechanism activated causing the gate to slide open. Tundra returned to the car, fastened her seatbelt and they drove to the entrance of the prison.

As they exited, Super Penguin spoke up again, "As a reminder, we *still* don't have a plan."

"I know," Sam replied with both annoyance and stress in his voice. "I was hoping the plan would reveal itself to us or something." With uncertainty in his eyes, Sam frantically looked around to gather as much information as possible in a short amount of time.

From their current position, they could see the entirety of the south and west walls. There was nothing going on along the south wall; however, at the northwest corner, they noticed a semi-truck hauling...

something. Outside the truck was a shorter someone. Sam pulled out a pair of binoculars and looked at the being.

Super Penguin, still behind him, snarked, "A periscope probably would have been cheaper."

Sam ignored him and kept looking.

"Is a monocular a thing?" Super Penguin continued, "it *sounds* like a thing that exists. You should look into one...you know, because the one eye...you don't need both...nobody's laughing! C'mon guys that was funny!"

The lion pulled the binoculars away from his face, "It's the pig! Alright, think, think, think. Do we engage him now, out here, or try to ambush him inside? What's his plan?"

BOOM!

An explosion went off a few feet from the semi-truck. Sam put the binoculars back up to his face. As he looked, he noticed Dr. Pigg walking away from the explosion and back to the truck's liftgate. Then, Dr. Pigg opened the liftgate.

Sam gasped, "This isn't good."

"What is it?" Tundra replied.

"That truck is filled with DragonCorp robots. It looks like five, no six across. I can't see how far back it goes, but there's *a lot* of them!"

"Okay," Sam's plan had appeared. "We aren't going to catch them if we run to where they are from here, so instead we need to cut them off where they are going to be. Hopefully, we meet the others inside. We won't be able to take them all on!"

The crew entered the building. Super Penguin equipped his staff and twisted it to engage the electric component.

Sam led the way, explaining his thought process to the team along the way. "The most dangerous criminals are kept on the lower levels and towards the center." After a few turns, the crew met a swarm of bots. It wasn't the full invasion, just a small pod of them. Sam turned to his friends, "There's more out there. Tundra and I will slow these ones down. Kid, get to Talon! Straight down that hallway!

Super Penguin obeyed and sprinted down the hall. The penguin continued to hold his weapon. He kept expecting to run into more bots, the Garbage Gang or *somebody* as he got closer to Talon, but he was wrong. The halls were quiet, too quiet. Something was wrong. Was this a trap? He continued along the path.

When Super Penguin arrived, Talon was still in his cell. The Komodo dragon, having traded in his three-piece designer suits for an orange jump suit, was now lying in bed, reading a tattered copy of *How to Make Friends and Impact People* by Dale Canary. The reptile's eyes left the page and moved to the penguin. "Oh," Talon spoke as he lowered the book. "I wasn't expecting any visitors. Is there anything I can help you with Mr. Super Penguin?"

"Yeah right, Talon! There's a massive break in going on all around, and you don't know anything about it?"

The lizard smirked, rose to his feet and approached the penguin.

"Look here, little bird. I know you're a smart guy. If I didn't hate you so much for ruining my life, I'd admire you quite a bit. But right now, you're looking pretty foolish."

Super Penguin's intense stare morphed into a confused stupor. "What...what do you mean?"

"We've not known each other very long, little bird, but in our short time as adversaries you proved to learn a lot about me. Would you say that's correct?"

"Um...okay?"

"Now, take all that you know about me in that little bird brain of yours and tell me. Can you think of one soul who would want to break me out of here?"

"Well, I…"

"The answer is a very obvious 'of course there isn't, and while I still despise you and would love to see you fail, I also don't want to see anyone else taking over *my* city." The lizard sat back down, grabbed his book, and began to recline into his original position. "I presume this is the gorilla's doing. You'll want to find him. If he's still where I left him, he should be in the second, no I think it was the third sub-level. Your police dog friend will know."

"Wha…how do you know all this?"

"You're running out of time, little bird." As he said this, Talon redirected all his attention back to his book. "Now, where was I?" he muttered to himself.

***

Super Penguin rushed back to where he had left his peers. As he ran through the halls, he thought to himself, "What on earth is going on? What is Talon hiding? And who the heck is this gorilla?" When he returned to the rendezvous point, there was one robot left but not for long. Sam swung his cane like a baseball slugger swings his bat right into the robot's head. The blow decapitated the bot, and the head crashed into the wall with a burst of sparks and smoke.

"Okay, first off, that was awesome! Nice swing, boss-man! Second thing, this isn't about Talon. Well, maybe he's involved, I don't really know what's going on, but he's trying to help us. I don't know why he's trying to help us…"

"Supes! Focus!" Tundra bellowed.

"Sorry! Deputy Boone, he said something about a gorilla being the target for the breakout. He said you'd know all about it."

"A gorilla?" Boone questioned, scratching behind his ear as he thought. "I can only think of one."

"In the lower levels?" Paul added.

"Yeah, that's just below where we are now. He's been in a coma for months. Not a lot of guards in that area. This way!" The dog led the group to the stairwell. Boone, Super Penguin, Tundra, and a hobbling Sam made their way down the three flights of stairs into the medical ward of the prison. They took a couple of turns, and when they arrived in the gorilla's room, they met a small crowd. The fox, skunk and raccoon that were at DragonCorp were helping the now conscious gorilla out of bed. Meanwhile, Dr. Pigg was laying belly-up on the floor with two robots standing beside his unconscious body. Super Penguin pulled out his staff and extended it to its fighting position. The Garbage Gang and robots charged towards the heroes. The skunk and raccoon charged at Tundra, a robot each ran at Boone and Sam, and the fox moved

towards Super Penguin.

The fox swiped once with his right paw and then his left. Super Penguin ducked under both and struck the fox in the rib cage with his staff.

"Argh!" the fox yelled out and pounced at the penguin. Super Penguin dodged to his left, out of the way, and in his peripheral, he noticed Sam was down and now two robots were teaming against Boone. The noises behind him suggested that Tundra was holding up fine. Super Penguin tried to make his purple glow return. He thrust his flippers away from himself, as if to ignite something from within, but nothing happened. He tried twice more before the fox

was back for more attacks. Super Penguin dodged and got a couple more blows in, but the fox was unrelenting. If anything, the penguin was agitating the fox which led to him moving faster with every jab of the staff. The dodges became less and less effective. Super Penguin began to grow tired and was losing. He tried one more time to force his power out, and again he failed. Suddenly, the skunk was flung across the room and into the fox knocking them both unconscious. Super Penguin turned towards where the skunk came from and saw Tundra had saved him.

After scanning the room, Super Penguin noticed Boone had helped Sam leave the room, and Tundra had finished off everyone but the gorilla, who had been letting the others battle. The gorilla let out a war cry, pounded his fists on his chest and then charged at Tundra. She reared back her right arm and readied a punch. She stepped forward as the gorilla charged and unleashed a devastating blow right to the gorilla's face. Super Penguin watched in amazement as the gorilla dropped to the ground, unconscious once again.

"Wow, Annie, that was incredible!"

Tundra looked confused, as if she wasn't quite sure what just happened. Super Penguin noticed immediately that something was off. "Annie, are you okay?"

"Me?"

"Yeah...are we still doing this? *Tundra!* Are you okay, *Tundra?*"

"Tundra?"

"Maybe not the best time to joke around. *Are you okay?*"

"Yeah...I'm...I'm good." She flicked her paw in a few directions to ease the pain.

Boone came back into the room. "Good work, you two! Sam's sitting in the other room. He hurt his bad leg in the scuffle. I'll call this in, and we'll get these guys all out of here and into custody. "I'll wrap this up. You guys get out of here before the press shows up."

"Alright," Super Penguin replied and then turned to Tundra. "I'm starving! Let's help Sam get out of here, and then do you want to grab dinner?"

"Sure. Where are you thinking?"

"Um...Tina's...the place we always go...are you sure you're okay?"

"Yeah, yeah, I'm fine. Let's go there."

***

Super Penguin had changed into his regular clothes before dinner and now Paul sat across from Sam at their usual booth at Tina's diner. The two had been waiting for Annie for nearly fifteen minutes.

"What is taking her so long?" Paul asked with annoyance in his voice. "She left when we did!"

"She seemed pretty shook up." Sam replied. "She's probably just taking a few extra minutes to collect herself. You in some kind of hurry or something?"

"No," Paul's annoyance faded. "I think I'm just hangry. Oh, there she is! Why is she looking around? We always sit here." The penguin's volume increased as he shouted across the restaurant. "Over here, Annie!" he shouted while waving.

The bear hurriedly walked to their table and slid in next to Paul.

"You okay?" Paul asked his friend.

"Yeah," she answered shortly, "I'm fine."

Tina, an ostrich and the owner of the restaurant, saw that the remainder of the party had arrived and came over to take their order.

"Black coffee and the fish sandwich for me," Sam ordered.

"The usual for me!" Paul said as he handed Tina the menu he never opened.

Tina jotted onto her notepad and replied, "That's the Anchovy Club, extra anchovies, and a water. Same for you, Annie?"

"I'll have the banana cream pie and a side order of bananas, please."

Tina, Sam, and Paul's mouths all dropped open in unison as they couldn't believe what they had just heard.

The ostrich crossed off what she presumed Annie was going to order and walked away. Paul spoke up, "Annie, are you *sure* you're okay?"

"Yes, I'm fine. Why do you ask?"

"Why do I ask? We've been here thousands of times going all the way back since before we were in high school. Of those thousands of visits, we've always sat in the same seats, and you've always ordered one thing and one thing only."

"I...just wanted to try something different I guess."

"Try something different?" Paul was about to go off on a tangent but was stopped by Sam.

"Alright, that's enough about that. I don't always order the same thing. If she wanted to try something new, then she's certainly allowed to do that without you getting all weird about it. Besides, we should be celebrating. You two stopped a major prison break and captured everyone involved. This should be a happy dinner!"

Paul didn't respond, bit his tongue, and didn't bring up his friend's odd behavior for the rest of the meal.

After the meal, they paid their bills and went their separate ways. Paul made his way to his car where he found a small, folded piece of paper under his car's windshield wiper. The penguin retrieved it, unfolded the note, and found there was nothing written on the paper. He flipped it over and held it up to the light but still found no message. "Who puts a blank note on a car?" he said aloud, presumably to himself.

"I do," a mysterious voice replied.

Paul looked around but could not figure out where the voice had originated.

"Ahem, down here." Paul looked down and saw a gray rat wearing a white robe.

"When you didn't respond to my first note, I presumed you could not read."

The penguin chuckled. "Wow, that's rude. I'm glad I blew you off then."

"I apologize. I am not one to dabble in sarcasm, and my presumption was honest; though, now I realize it could be deemed offensive. Please, let me introduce myself.   I am Master Chee."

"Nice to meet you Chee..."

"Master Chee," the rat corrected.

"Sorry, ahem, nice to meet you *Master* Chee."

"It is nice to meet you, as well. I am here to invite you to my island where I train gifted individuals, such as yourself."

"Hey man, I mean, Master. It's been a really weird day for me. Well, it's been weirder than a typical day. Can we set up a meeting or something? Maybe something a little more private than outside a diner?"

"Very well. I will return tomorrow evening, but I will need a decision at that point. I will meet you at your home."

"How do you know where I live? You know what, don't answer that. It's probably better I don't know...that's fine. I'll see you tomorrow, Master Chee."

The rat nodded toward the penguin, turned around, and waved his hand in a clockwise circular motion. As he did, a bright, white light appeared also in the shape of a circle. Chee stepped into the light, and he quickly disappeared with the light disappearing immediately after him.

Paul pinched himself. "Nope, that was real," he said aloud. "This has been one weird day." The penguin shook himself from his head to his toes, as if to rid himself of the weirdness and then got into his car and drove home.

* * *

Paul stood outside the camouflaged door of Sam's hideout waiting for his watch to hit exactly 5 a.m. When it did, the door appeared, and Sam let his friend inside. "Where's Annie?" Sam asked.

"She's not here? She's always here before me. I'll call her right now." Paul pulled his phone out of his pocket and called Annie, but there was no answer. "It went to voicemail. What do you think happened to her?"

"I don't know," the lion paused to take a sip of his coffee. "I know someone else who's also been acting odd, so maybe it's contagious." Sam glared at his friend. "You ready to talk about your thing yet? Or are you keeping secrets, too?"

"Well, I mean...I'm not actively trying to avoid it...I'm just still processing. But I guess talking it out with a friend couldn't hurt. So, remember when you and I fought Talon in that alley?"

"Ha!"

"Okay, of course you remember. I..um..." the penguin was running out of words to stall the conversation. "This is going to sound crazy, so be warned...and no I didn't make it up, or have a weird dream, or get hit in the head."

Sam didn't utter a word or make a facial expression. He just looked on and listened. Paul continued, "So, after you collapsed, this.... um... this weird purple energy came out of my body, and when I hit Talon with my staff, it was extra powerful. That's what took him down. I have no idea where it came from, but someone did, and they left me a note at the newspaper office. This mysterious somebody wanted me to meet them back in the alley where it happened, but that seemed like a bad idea, so I didn't. Then, last night after Tina's, this rat showed up saying he sent me the note, and he wants me to train on his secret island. Then he disappeared in this portal thing."

Sam's eyebrows narrowed, "Are you sure you didn't get hit in the head?"

"SAM!"

"Alright, alright, I'm sorry. That's just...a lot to process."

"No kidding, man! I didn't know how to tell you two about what was going on because I didn't even know what the heck was going on!"

"So, what's your plan?"

"What do you mean?"

"Are you going to train with him? If he has some kind of superpowers, he probably *could* teach you about yours."

"Yeah, but I have no idea how long I'd be gone. Annie's acting weird, and with the prison break out attempt and the DragonCorp break in, is now the right time?

"Kid, I don't know that there will ever be a convenient time to go, but as the bad guys get stronger and stronger, it's not a bad idea for you to have a secret weapon."

"Yeah, you're right. That Garbage Gang was pretty tough. If it weren't for Annie, I would have been a goner."

"So, it's settled. How do you get in touch with this rat?"

"He said he'd meet me at my apartment later tonight."

"How does he know...?"

"I don't know," Paul interrupted his friend, "and I'm not sure I want to know how he knows."

Sam nodded in agreement and then felt his phone buzz in his pocket. The lion pulled it out and read to himself. "Seriously?" he exclaimed. "That Junk Jamboree escaped custody!"

Confused, Paul asked "The Junk Jamboree? Are you talking about the Garbage Gang?"

"Yeah, them! Boone says the squad car that was bringing them back to the station was ambushed. The deputy that was driving them was sitting at a red light. Then, all of a sudden, his door was ripped off, and he was knocked out by a punch. When he came to, the perps were gone."

"I'm sure that won't be the last we see of them!"

***

The Garbage Gang's hideout was exactly what you'd expect from a group who named themselves "The Garbage Gang." It was in an abandoned warehouse that was well past its prime. The exterior included some broken windows and others that were boarded over with plywood. What was once the loading dock was now a pile of old desks, chairs, and various pieces of warehouse equipment the Garbage Gang had shoved out to make space inside. Of the two loading doors, only the left one still opened or closed, manually of course, since the building's power had been shut off many years before.

Inside the hideout, some of the bigger equipment was still in place either because they were bolted down or were too heavy for the four creatures to push. Near the center of the warehouse were offices that had been turned into bedrooms. There were three smaller ones for the opossum, raccoon and skunk, and a larger room that belonged to the fox. The skunk, raccoon and fox had gathered in the fox's room to forage over a box of stolen DragonCorp's technology.

"Hey Arthur, look at this thing!" The skunk said to the fox as he held up a golden belt adorned with colorful wires, switches, and buttons. The raccoon quickly swiped it from the skunk.

"Give me that, Stinky!" said the raccoon to the skunk.

The skunk immediately tried to swipe it back but missed. "Hey, I found that first, Rocko!" the skunk whined. "And quit calling me Stinky!"

Arthur Dodge, the fox, tried to settle the dispute before it escalated further. "Okay, you two. Big Boss said there's enough tech here for each of us to take one thing, and we'll get more when the penguin isn't watching so closely." Arthur turned to the skunk, "Here, Lester, this looks like something you'd like," he said as the fox handed the skunk a pair of silver boots also adorned with several wires, switches, and buttons. "Try them on and see what they do."

Meanwhile, the fox pulled out a pair of white, hard, plastic gauntlets. The exterior of the gauntlets was polished, and of the three devices, these were the furthest along. Arthur put them on, his right arm first and then his left. A strap wrapped around each of his paws, and there was a single, small, red button conveniently placed for his thumb. The fox stepped into the hallway, pointed his right gauntlet down the corridor and pushed the red button. A small door opened on the top of the gauntlet, and a small cannon-like device emerged. Then, a pulse of sonic energy shot out of the small cannon. As it travelled down the hallway, the sonic wave grew larger in diameter. As it travelled, the wave let out a loud, booming tone. Glass windows in the wave's path shattered, and as the wave got bigger, it's sound became less potent and eventually dissipated.

Rocko, the raccoon, hollered from the room, "That was pretty cool Arthur, but check this out!" When the fox turned, he saw Rocko wearing the gold belt. He had lifted the fox's desk and was holding it in the air with one paw. "Pretty cool, huh? Yo! Lester, what do your boots do?"

The skunk had just finished fastening the boots and had started flipping switches. "They aren't doing anything!"

Arthur, now back in the room and taking off his sonic gauntlets, replied, "Surely, they do something. Try moving around in them."

Lester walked in place. Nothing. He ran in place. Still nothing. Then, he tried a jump. Lester bent his knees, and when he straightened and leapt upwards, the ground shook as he was propelled through the drop ceiling and up through the next two floors before he came crashing back down. Delirious, the skunk smiled and let out a, "That was awesome," before he collapsed, but when he did, he let out his skunk smell and sprayed into the room!

"Dang it, Lester!" Arthur howled as he and Rocko left the room and closed the door behind them. The two coughed and waved the stench away from their noses. As they composed themselves, Arthur's cell phone began to ring. He looked at the caller ID where "BIG BOSS" displayed for the contact's name.

"Boss is calling. I'd better get that!" He hit the green accept button, "Hey, boss! Good morning! Thanks again for keeping us out of prison. That little rescue mission of yours was pretty gutsy and very impressive!

"Did you get the equipment I sent?"

"Oh...haha...straight to business I see...yeah, we did, thank you..."

"Your next assignment will be in a few days. Lay low and get acquainted with the tech I sent you. I will contact you with further instructions."

"Alright...thanks boss...boss?" he pulled the phone from his ear and looked at the screen to see the call had ended. "Okay, seriously? You're hanging up on me? What a jerk!"

Rocko, who had been listening nearby, said, "So we're supposed to just hang out here and wait?"

"No way," replied Arthur, "Wake up, Stinky. We're going out!"

***

BZZT BZZT BZZT

Paul answered, "Hey, Boone. What's up?"

"We've got a situation downtown. That Trash Troup, or whatever their name is, is downtown causing a bunch of havoc. Looks like they have some gizmos. If you and Tundra aren't too busy, we could use a hand!"

"Where are you?"

"Downtown. Just outside the movie theater."

"That's just a couple blocks over. I'll be there in a few minutes!" Paul pulled out his cell phone and while he began to collect his gear and put on his uniform, he called Annie. Brrrring Brrrrring Briiiing. No answer, and the voicemail box was full. "Annie! Where the heck are you?" he muttered to himself. The penguin was now in his full Super Penguin uniform and headed for the door when he suddenly remembered his last run in with his neighbor Gary. "I should probably stop using the front door," he advised himself. Instead, he left his apartment using the fire escape outside his bedroom window. The penguin moved his way down the ladders and into the alleyway next to the building's dumpsters. No sooner did Super Penguin's feet hit the ground when he heard the dumpster cover slam open.

"Paul? Is that you?"

Super Penguin turned around to see his neighbor, Gary, once again. He didn't know what to say, so he blankly stared.

"Still wearing your cosplay, I see!" the gazelle began to tease. "Man, I knew you were weird, but this is a new level!" He threw his bag of trash into the dumpster, closed the lid with another loud slam of the cover, and chuckled as he left the alley.

It took a moment for the confused look to leave Super Penguin's face. He asked himself, "How has he not pieced this together?" No time to ponder. Super Penguin made his way to the movie theater.

The streets were busy, and traffic was at a standstill. As he ran down the sidewalk, he heard some honking and yelling from the vehicles and the occasional, "Hey! Look! It's Super Penguin!" He even passed a young penguin with his parents. The child's face lit up with excitement! "Mommy! Daddy! It's him!"

Super Penguin arrived at the scene to find the Garbage Gang acting more chaotically than ever. The south end of the road where Super Penguin stood was barricaded by police cars. Many citizens had evacuated the block, but some were trapped in buildings in the middle. Cars and trucks were parked along each side of the street. The police were firing their laser pistols (a weapon made by the *original* DragonCorp that would stun but not otherwise harm the target) with little success. They ducked from behind their car barricade, peaked over the top, fired off a few shots and ducked behind again. The Garbage Gang's new tech was overpowering. The skunk was leaping high into the air and crashing down, dodging the ranged attacks and whacking cops with a punch or kick before leaping back into the air. The raccoon had picked up a yellow taxicab and was using it to shield himself and the fox from the laser fire while the fox was shooting sonic waves back at the police.

The police had to pause to cover their ears and brace themselves before they could fire back. Glass from the windows had shattered all over the pavement.

Super Penguin found Boone taking cover behind one of the middle police cars, so the penguin started there.

"Thank goodness you're here!" Boone said when his friend approached.

"You got a plan?"

"Yeah, stop those guys!" the dog sarcastically yelled. "We're open to suggestions on how to do that though!"

Super Penguin scoffed and scanned the scene. Just ahead, he saw Annie in her Tundra gear watching the mayhem. The penguin hero made his way toward his partner, ducking behind mailboxes, trash cans and other obstacles along the way to avoid being seen by the Garbage Gang.

"*Psst Tundra!*"

"Wh...what are you doing here?"

"Um.... saving the city...remember the superhero thing we signed up for?"

Tundra wasn't amused and didn't respond.

Super Penguin continued, "You nervous or something?"

"Yeah," Tundra replied, but she seemed to be hiding something. Super Penguin could tell something was wrong, but with everything else happening around them, his friend's feelings weren't a priority at the moment.

"Alright, I could really use your help, but if you need a minute to work up your courage...or whatever is going on...wait here and do that... but you're kinda the strongest animal in the city, so...don't take too long." Super Penguin patted his friend on the back as he moved to the other end of the car. He darted behind another car and then another, moving closer and closer to the raccoon and fox. After a little more sneaking, Super Penguin was perpendicular to the raccoon and fox, and they had not yet detected him. The penguin took out one of his smoke bombs and his retractable staff. With one flipper, he flicked his wrist and extended his weapon into fighting position. Just as he stepped into the street...

"HEY!" Tundra yelled toward him. This got the attention of the Garbage Gang and Arthur Dodge turned and fired a sonic blast at Super Penguin. Our hero dove back around the car and narrowly avoided the blast.

Super Penguin looked back to his friend "WHAT THE HECK WAS THAT, ANNIE?"

"I thought they saw you."

"WELL, THEY DID NOW!"

Sonic blasts now alternated between being shot towards the police barricade and Super Penguin.

Every time Super Penguin poked his head above the car, the fox shot off another sonic blast in his direction.

Tundra poked her head above the car to see the carnage. This surprised Dodge, and he reactively fired a sonic shot that hit her square in the head. The bear fell to the ground beyond the cover of the car.

"Annie!" Super Penguin yelled. The penguin stayed behind the car, but his attention was on his friend. Her chest was still moving, proving she was down but still alive. Super Penguin returned his attention back to the fox, who seemingly had forgotten all about the penguin in such a short amount of time. This was his chance. Super Penguin charged, and just like the day he fought Talon, a purple energy began to flow through him. This time was different. There was more energy, and it seemed to flow faster and stronger than before. Super Penguin was halfway to the fox when he leapt towards him. As he went into the air, the penguin grasped his staff with both wings and swung it from behind his head. The energy transferred from him to one end of the staff and then towards the tip that would soon hit the fox. Dodge had just a moment to react and was able to dive out of the way. The staff struck the concrete. When it did, a gigantic blast shot in a hemisphere with the penguin at its core. The Garbage Gang flew backwards and didn't get up. The few remaining intact windows shattered, and every car alarm on the block started blaring.

Super Penguin looked around at the aftermath. First, he saw the Garbage Gang. They were all knocked unconscious, and the DragonCorp technology they were wearing was now sparking. Next, he saw the spectators around the scene. They all had looks of fear on their faces. The police should have looked relieved that the threat had been taken down, but instead their faces were covered with looks of concern. They stared at Super Penguin in disbelief. Boone was the first to move and worked to get his men to leave their positions and apprehend the Garbage Gang. The last thing Super Penguin saw was Tundra, still on the ground. Super Penguin ran to her.

By the time he got to her, she had regained consciousness but was struggling to sit up. Tundra whispered, "Help...Me."

"I'm right here, Annie. What do you need?" Super Penguin replied worriedly. "What's wrong? How can I help?"

"I'm...not...GET AWAY FROM ME!" her mood quickly shifted. Tundra propped herself up and scooted away. A few seconds ago, she seemed exhausted, and suddenly it was like a great surge of energy had rejuvenated her. Super Penguin was understandably confused.

"Annie, what's wrong? I..."

"GET AWAY FROM ME!" she yelled again as she rose to her feet. She shoved Super Penguin back and ran down into an alleyway.

Stunned, Super Penguin just watched her leave.

***

You've reached the voicemail box of Annie Freese. I'm unable to get to the phone ri...

Paul ended the call. It had been several hours since the incident. Over the past two hours, he had already left four texts, and had made three phone calls. No answers or call backs. The penguin felt guilty for hurting his friend but confused at the same time. Why was she acting so weird? Maybe she couldn't handle the pressure of being Tundra. Paul had a mostly positive experience becoming a superhero, but that didn't mean she would too. He thought to himself, *Maybe Sam's talked to her...I'll give him a call.* Paul dialed the lion's number. It rang several times before also going to voicemail. He ended the call and heard a *knock, knock, knock* at his door. It was Master Chee. He had nearly forgotten his appointment. Paul answered the door. His presumption was correct as there in front of him was the rat he had met once before.

"Hello, Mr. Frost. Have you thought more about my offer?"

"Yeah." The penguin had made up his mind, but he still wasn't sure it was the right decision especially now that Annie was upset with him, and he hadn't talked to her about his departure. "Come on in."

The rat nodded and obeyed. Paul shut the door behind him and said, "When does the next round of classes start?"

"Tomorrow."

"Tomorrow? I haven't packed..."

"That won't be necessary. We have everything you need on the island."

"Okay, well, let me grab my phone charger..."

"That won't be necessary. You'll be leaving your phone here."

"Leave my phone? But what if..."

"Mr. Frost, you have no use for a cellular phone on my island."

"Oh, I see. This is one of those transcendental, philosophical camp-things where I can't be bogged down with technology?"

"No...we just don't have service on the island."

Paul awkwardly laughed, "Haha...that actually makes a lot of sense! Okay, let's do this."

The rat nodded, turned away from the penguin, and made the circular motion with his paw. A portal appeared in front of the door. Master Chee turned to face Paul and said, "Follow me, Mr. Frost." Then, he turned once more and walked through the portal. The penguin followed, and they both disappeared from the apartment.

***

Paul stepped through the portal with Chee. With just a few steps, he was transported from Eagle City to a beach. The sun was setting, and the sky was the prettiest collection of blue, orange, purple and red that he had ever seen. The sound and sight of the ocean waves crashing onto the shore made it that much more beautiful.

"This place is beautiful!" Paul exclaimed. "It's like a picture from a postcard! Where are we?"

"We are approximately 3000 miles southwest of the coast of Newt Jersey." Chee replied matter-of-factly.

"Sorry," the penguin chuckled, "I forgot how literally you take everything I say. What's the name of the island?"

"The island has no name, Mr. Frost. It just...exists. I suppose, if you must call it something, you can call it 'Chee's Island'."

Paul erupted in laughter. "Ha! Did you just say, 'Cheese Island'?"

"Yes," the rat tilted his head in confusion. "That's exactly what I said. Is something wrong?"

Realizing the rat still didn't have a sense of humor, Paul's laugh dissipated. "No, no, nothing wrong at all." The penguin looked around and noticed some grass huts behind them. He fought back more laughter when he asked, "So, is that the Cheese School?"

"Yes, it is. We will go there now. Please follow me." The rat led, and the penguin followed. As he walked, Paul continued to enjoy the sunset.

"I really can't get over how beautiful this place is! I've lived in Eagle City my whole life. I don't think I've ever seen a palm tree before in person, and I've definitely never walked on sand before, and that sunset...just wow."

The rat stopped at the first hut at the edge of the camp. "This is where you will stay. You will find a pillow and blanket inside. Is there anything else you'll need?"

Paul snickered, "Is there a wi-fi password?"

"I do not know what that means."

"Right, no jokes...I'm good, thank you, Master Chee."

"Good night, Mr. Frost."

Paul entered his hut. The pillow and blanket weren't hard to find as they were two of only three things in the hut, the third being a small bronze lantern with a candle emitting light. "Minimalists, I take it," he muttered to himself. The penguin laid down onto the sand, adjusted his pillow and covered himself with the blanket before blowing out the lantern.

***

When Paul woke up, the sun was shining. He stood, dusted the sand off of himself, and walked outside. The scene was just as beautiful as the day before, and a gentle breeze accompanied the marvelous sight. Paul looked around and saw the silhouettes of four creatures down by the beach where he had arrived yesterday. He walked in that direction. As he got closer, he recognized Chee with three other animals in front of him- a small, yellow canary, a corgi that was about his height, and a chameleon who was a little taller than Paul. Each of the four wore an all-white outfit that he had only seen in karate movies.

As the penguin approached, they appeared to be meditating. Paul whispered, "Hey, Master Chee. Sorry, I'm late."

The rat opened one of his eyes and looked in the penguin's direction.

Paul continued, "I didn't know what time this started. Was there a robe for me in my hut? I didn't see one..."

"Karategi," the corgi interjected as she broke her concentration and was now staring at Paul.

"I'm sorry? I don't speak...whatever language that was..."

"Our uniform. It's called a 'karategi,' and you must earn it before you receive it, penguin."

Chee stood, though being a rat, it was hard to tell. "That's enough, Nula, thank you." He turned his attention to Paul, "Mr. Frost, good morning. We begin each day when the sun rises. If you are late, you move wood."

"What does that mean?"

The rat pointed behind Paul down to the north of the island. "There is a pile of wood at the northern tip. Please bring it here."

Paul turned to look at where the rat was pointing, a scene he could not see the night before. Beyond the camp, the ground slowly sloped upward to a small mountain.

"All the way up there?" Paul asked. "Isn't there wood near the camp or...somewhere not up that mountain?"

"Mr. Frost," the rat gave a look of disapproval.

Paul sighed and turned to the mountain. When he got out of earshot of Master Chee, he began to rant, "This is so stupid! How the heck was I supposed to know his class started at sunrise? Didn't give me a schedule, no alarm clock, not even a mention of when anything was happening..." Paul went on like this for most of the hike. The sun beat down on him as he climbed for several hours. As the penguin reached the summit, the sun was at its highest point, and there was very little shade. Paul noticed a single, short log laying on a red blanket. He walked towards it, and when close enough he bent over and picked it up. The bark was gone and carved into it was a short message that read, *No matter how strenuous the task, make sure to stop and enjoy the view. -Chee.* The penguin looked up from the log and was mesmerized. He thought yesterday's view from the beach was the most beautiful sight he had ever seen, but the view today, on top of the mountain was even more captivating. Paul tucked the log under his wing and made his way back the way he came. His mood had drastically improved, and as he walked, he kept looking at the view and couldn't help but smile.

When Paul returned to the starting point, it was nearly sunset. Only Master Chee was waiting for him. "How was your hike, Mr. Frost?"

"It was...nice." He smiled as he took the wood from under his wing and presented it to the rat.

"And what lesson did you learn?"

"This island has a pretty sweet view!"

"I'm afraid you missed the point, Mr. Frost."

"What do you mean? I got up there and saw the view! It was remarkable, really! I'm not just saying that. I admired it the whole way down."

"But why did it take you to the top of the summit to notice the beautiful scenery? Was it not there for your entire hike?"

"I...I guess it was..."

"Mr. Frost, every journey is like a hike up a mountain. It's difficult. It's hard. You won't reach every summit, *but* if you are paying attention, you can see the beauty of every hike, even the most strenuous ones. You have a very large mountain ahead of you as *Super Penguin*, a hike so long that you likely won't ever reach the summit. Make sure you appreciate the journey while you're going through it, not just at the top. That's it for today's lesson." As Chee finished, he waved his paws, opening a portal. Then the rat tossed the log back onto the blanket.

The penguin chuckled, "That was a really moving lesson and all...but watching you do that portal thing after making me climb a mountain...kinda frustrating."

Chee cracked a smile. "See you tomorrow, Mr. Frost."

Paul made his way back to his hut. Once inside, he noticed a small white box tied with a piece of twine fashioned into a bow. On top of the box was a note. The penguin curiously opened the note and read, "I hope this helps you get to class on time, and remember, I hear everything. From: Master Chee." Paul set the note down, pulled on the bow and opened the package to find a battery powered alarm clock, his own karategi, and a hand-written schedule of events for the following day. "Pretty creepy, Chee...pretty cool trick, but pretty creepy."

***

Paul's second morning on the island started with the ringing of his alarm clock. He shot up and looked outside the hut. It was still dark. He cleaned himself up and headed to the beach. Though he had beaten the sun, he appeared to be the last student on the beach as Master Chee and the three others he saw the morning before were all there. "Good morning, Mr. Frost. I'm glad to see you up this early."

"Thanks," the penguin said as he yawned.

"I don't believe you've met the other students, "Chee said as he motioned towards the corgi, chameleon, and canary. "This is Nula. She was one of my very first students and continues to train with me." He then motioned to the chameleon, "This is Blank. He's been training with us for about a year. And this is Pip," Master Chee said now motioning toward the canary, "he's the youngest student I've ever trained."

"It's nice to meet you all!" Paul replied. He shook hands with each classmate and then asked Pip, "You seem awfully young to be out here. Your parents were okay with you leaving home and being out here?"

"Well, sir, I didn't know my parents. I hatched here. I was told Master Chee found my egg and brought me here."

Chee grimaced, but only Paul could see. The penguin thought to himself, *There's more to that story but not in front of the kid.* After the pleasantries were exchanged, Paul inquired, "I don't mean to sound rude, or ask any uncomfortable questions, but...do you three have that purple energy coming out of you too?"

Nula spoke for the group, "Not quite. We all have different powers."

"So can we do like a superpower show and tell?" Paul asked.

The other students looked to Chee who gave a nod of approval.

Simultaneously, Blank disappeared while a transparent and translucent sphere shrouded around Nula.

"Where did Blank go?"

"I'm still here," Blank replied despite being nowhere to be seen. "I'm just invisible."

"That's pretty cool! Nula, what's your orb thing do?"

"It's an energy shield. While I have this up, nothing can go through it."

"Nice, nice," an amused Paul said as he nodded his head with excitement. He looked to Pip, "And what about you?"

Pip's mouth didn't move, but Paul could hear his voice say, "I'm a telepath!" The voice sounded like it was coming from *inside* Paul's head.

"Okay, this is freaky!" Paul shouted, "but really stinking cool at the same time. Can you read my mind and stuff?"

Pip's voice was now emitting from his own body. "Master Chee says he thinks I will be able to someday, but for now it's just sending messages. I can move some things with my mind, too!"

"Um, did you just say you can move thing's with your mind? What kind of things?"

Pip didn't answer with words. He demonstrated his ability by lifting his left wing towards Paul and closing his eyes. Seconds later, the penguin began to float. He was two feet off the ground when he suddenly dropped. Pip fell to the ground too.

As Paul's feet hit the sand, he went to aid Pip, "You okay, kid?"

"Yeah, sometimes it takes a lot out of me to use my power."

Master Chee approached and put a hand on the canary's back "Pip, you must remember not to push yourself too hard. You're very young, and your mind is still developing. The power inside of you will get stronger, and your endurance will build too, but you must take things slow."

"Yes, Master Chee," the canary responded as he rose to his feet.

Blank reappeared and looked to the penguin. "Alright, we showed you what we can do. Your turn!"

Paul's cheeks grew red, and he began to scratch the back of his head with his wing. "Well, I…um…."

Chee interrupted again. "Mr. Frost is just learning how to control his powers. That is why he is here, and that will be the subject of today's lesson. We will be sparring…"

"Yes!" exclaimed Pip, who immediately received a disapproving glance from Chee. "Sorry. Sparring's just my favorite."

"You are forgiven, young one. Pip, you'll spar with Blank. I'd like you to go to the mountain for your sparring session. Nula and Paul, you'll be partners. You'll spar right here." Blank and Pip followed their orders and left the group.

Paul raised his wing, "Um, my power has only come out twice, and both times it was on accident…and I don't even have my staff."

"Do you believe the staff will help?"

"Well…I don't really know…but it's always been there when the power came out."

"Hmm…interesting" Chee replied. The rat opened a portal beside him, reached into it and pulled out Paul's weapon.

"Wait…were you just in my room?"

Chee didn't respond to the question. Instead, he grabbed each end of the staff and snapped it over his knee breaking it in half.

"WHAT DID YOU DO THAT FOR?" Paul yelled as he dove towards the two broken pieces and tried to piece them back together while he kneeled in the sand.

Chee put his paw on the penguin's shoulder, "Your power doesn't come from the staff, Mr. Frost."

"Well, then were *does* it come from? Your note said you knew, but you still haven't told me!"

"It comes from…inside you, Mr. Frost."

"INSIDE ME? THAT'S YOUR BIG REVEAL! I'VE GOT FRIENDS AT HOME COUNTING ON ME, MY BEST FRIEND WON'T TALK TO ME, MY MENTOR HAS GONE MISSING…"

"Paul…" Nula called and nodded her head towards his clenched fists. They were glowing purple.

Paul looked down at the glow, but after a few seconds it disappeared.

"See, no special electronic staff needed, but here, try this." Chee tossed Paul a traditional wooden bō staff. The staff was made of oak and had been sanded for a smooth finish. In the center of the staff, a cloth strap wrapped around for Paul to grip it with ease. Paul examined the staff and twirled it around a few times. "Have you discovered where the power originates Mr. Frost?"

"I mean...not really..."

"Think about your feelings and your emotions...how do you feel when the power appears?"

"Well, the first time was when I fought Talon...and then the Garbage Gang...and now from being angry at you..."

"So, you believe anger is the source?"

"I...I think so?"

"Well, let's see it then. Nula, you'll be on defense. Paul, you may attack once your power is armed but not before. The penguin began to think of every angry thought he could bring to his mind, but nothing happened. He began to get angrier because his anger wasn't working. His face began to turn red, and he let out a primal scream, "AAAAAGGHHHHH WHY ISN'T THIS WORKING?"

"Mr. Frost let's re-examine your feelings from the past when your power appeared. Your fight with Talon, walk me through what happened."

"I thought you were there and saw it all happen?"

"My memory is foggy. Please indulge me."

"Ok, well, Henry and I were fighting Talon, and then Henry left to get backup. Then, Sam showed up to help me, and then he went down..."

"There. Talk to me about Sam."

"He's my mentor and a friend..."

"He's someone you care about, yes?"

"Absolutely."

"Someone you love?"

"Of course. He's been like a father figure to me throughout the whole superhero thing."

"And when you fought the Garbage Gang the first time. Annie held her own, and your power didn't come out, but when she was hurt in the street, it did appear, correct? What are your feelings about Annie?"

"She's my best friend, like the sister I never had..."

"Mr. Frost, moments ago when your fists started to glow...they weren't glowing until you talked about your friends. Look at your wings again."

Paul looked down, and the purple glow had returned.

Chee continued, "Mr. Frost, that is the source of your power...and all of our powers here on my island. You thought your power came from anger, and anger *can* be very powerful. I believe your nemesis Talon's power came from anger. But the greatest power comes from love. Try focusing on that."

"Sounds kind of *Chee-sy*! Ha! See what I did there?"

Master Chee chuckled; it was the first time Paul had ever seen him crack a smile. "That was pretty funny, Mr. Frost. I'll have to remember that one. Now, let's get to work on honing your power."

Paul spent the next several hours sparring with Nula, learning how to manifest and control his power. They did not stop until the sun set over the horizon.

***

Paul was the first to the beach on morning number three, and he was there just before the sun was up. However, the sun came up, and nobody had joined him. He waited. "This is probably some kind of test" the penguin told himself. It was not. He stopped monologuing and instead sat and watched the sun rise over the mountain he had climbed days before. Paul was once again transfixed by the beauty of the island and sat almost as if he was in some sort of hypnotic trance. Though he was looking in that direction, he didn't see the canary, Pip, make his way towards him.

"Hey Paul!" the little bird exclaimed, genuinely happy to see him. "How are you today?"

"You know what? For being stranded on an island and having no idea where I am, I'm actually doing pretty darn well. This power was freaking me out, but now that I have some control over it, life's just a little less stressful."

"That's really good! Good job, Paul!"

"Thanks, Pip! So...nobody else is out here. What's up with that?"

"It's the weekend. We don't have class on the weekend."

The penguin laughed, "This place is great, but a schedule or an itinerary would be really helpful!"

"Oh yeah! I forgot! We haven't had anyone new for a while. Master Chee doesn't tell people anything. They have to learn it. He says it's some kind of lesson or something."

"So, he does this to everyone? That's a relief. I was beginning to think he just didn't like me."

"I think he likes you a lot!" the canary corrected. "You didn't have to build your own hut, and he put the special log up there on the first day for you! The last guy that came through here had to go get wood like three days in a row before the one with the carvings was up there."

"Interesting...was that Blank?"

"No, it was an alligator, but he wasn't green like most alligators. He was all white with blue eyes and really mean. He was actually Master Chee's first student, but he left and then he came back. His name was Xavier..."

"Ahem." Chee had used a portal to sneak behind them. "Pip, what have I told you about over sharing about past students?"

"Sorry, Master Chee. I forgot."

Chee patted the canary on the back and then spoke. "I know there's no class today, but I have a special lesson for just the two of you. Would you care to join me?"

"Yes!" Pip exclaimed.

Paul added with a laugh, "Well, I *was* planning on class today, since *someone* withheld that information, so I'm game!"

Chee made one of his portals and directed, "Please, follow me." The portal transported them to another island. This island didn't have sandy beaches or a collection of huts. It was one big rock with a cliff and only one way down. Chee left the portal open. "Your task for today is to fly home." He pointed to another island. "That's my island right there. I'll see you when you get back," and he began to step back into the portal.

The penguin spoke up, "Woah, woah, woah, wait a second. How are we supposed to get there?"

Chee answered matter-of-factly, "I just told you. You'll fly, of course."

Paul scoffed, "I don't fly. I'm a penguin."

"Penguins *can* fly." Chee replied sincerely.

"No, *we can't!*"

"I most certainly can assure you; penguins *do* fly."

"Chee...err, uhm Master Chee, with all due respect, penguins *don't* fly. I've seen several birds flapping their wings above Eagle City, and not one of them was a penguin. I can't fly. My parents couldn't fly. *Penguins don't fly!*"

Master Chee chuckled, "Why on earth would you look to the *sky* for penguins to fly? That's just ridiculous!"

"That's what I'm saying!"

"No, you said penguins don't fly. I said they don't fly in the *sky*." Paul looked at the rat with a confused stare, so Master Chee continued. "Penguins don't fly in the *sky*. They fly in the *water*."

"Yeah...that's called swimming," Paul retorted.

"I disagree. Your wing's motions resemble how all the other birds fly. You don't flap around like a fish."

"Well, I guess..."

"Mr. Frost, here is today's lesson. You are different from Pip. Pip is different from you. You've both been given the same task. You don't have to do things the exact same way as each other to be just as successful. You don't have to be like Pip to fly back to the island. You just have to be *you* and do it *your* way." Chee made his way into the portal and disappeared.

Paul stepped to the edge of the cliff, looked down at the water and said to himself, "Fly like a penguin, Paul. Fly like a penguin." His feet left the cliff, and the bird dove into the water majestically. When he reached the water, his beak cut through the waves with ease, and his body followed. He soared through the water with great speed. Like a fighter jet in a canyon, Paul steered himself around coral reefs, throwing in the occasional barrel roll for flair. A great, big smile was plastered on the penguin's face.

In a few minutes, he was back to Chee's Island. Paul reached the shallow water and began to walk the remainder of the way. Pip was descending not far behind. Just at the edge of the tide stood Master Chee. "Did you enjoy your flight, Mr. Frost?" Paul walked up to Chee and delivered a sopping wet hug. "I'll take that as a yes," Chee added as he embraced his student.

"Thank you," Paul said before breaking off the hug.

When the three returned to camp, they found Nula and Blank setting up an island barbeque. A small, healthy fire was cooking skewers of fish meat and vegetables. A wooden picnic table had been carried out to the beach, and it was adorned with island fruits that had been chopped and carefully arranged on a platter.

"Ah, just in time," Blank called out to his peers. "The food is just about done. Grab yourselves a plate!"

Paul and the others obeyed, each covering their plates with as much food as they could fit. Each member of the group found a place at the table. Blank started up the conversation. "So, Paul, what's home like for you?"

The penguin paused for a moment. It had been a while since he'd thought about his parents. So much had gone on in his adventures as Super Penguin that he had almost forgotten why he started fighting crime in the first place. "Well," he paused for a moment, "my mom and dad passed away awhile back...in a house fire..."

"I'm so sorry," Blank replied, "you don't have to talk about it if you don't want to. I was just trying to stir up some conversation."

Paul paused again. "It's okay. I don't like talking about the fire and how they died, but I can tell you how they lived."

Master Chee smiled at his student, "I would love to hear about that."

Paul smiled back, "Dad was doctor, a pediatrician to be exact. He loved helping kids get better. Mom was a science teacher. She was really smart. She had three degrees in education, biology, and geology! Meanwhile, I had a strong dislike for science, math, anatomy... pretty much everything science teachers and doctors are into!" Super Penguin laughed, and before he continued his story, he looked up at a cloud where he imagined his parents were sitting and watching him. He smiled and continued, "I really liked sports and writing. When I was about ten years old and learned that sportswriters existed, I knew that's what I wanted to do when I grew up. Mom and Dad both volunteered a lot, and they always brought me along. They helped everyone they could without expecting anything in return. I didn't realize it until now, but I think all that helping people made the version of me that would later become Super Penguin."

Blank inquired some more, "Do you have any brothers or sisters?"

"Just one sister. She's a polar bear."

The group shared a confused face. Nula added a "Huh?"

"Well, she's not *technically* my sister, but she might as well be. We grew up together. She's always been there for me when I needed her most, and I think I've always been there for her when she needed it too. Well, I thought that until recently. She's been acting distant, and I was distant before that because I didn't tell her about my powers. I'm sure when I get back, everything will be back to normal." Then Paul shared his story about becoming Super Penguin, fighting Talon and Annie becoming Tundra.

Nula was most impressed by Annie. "Your friend sounds awesome! She's fighting crime without powers. How brave!"

"I did that too! My power didn't show up until the end of the story, remember?"

"But you have them now, so it's not as cool." She smirked, knowing she had riled up Paul. "Just kidding, kid. You're alright too!"

After Paul shared his stories, the rest of the group shared their own. Everyone already knew Pip's, but they played along to entertain the kid and let him feel involved in the conversation. Then, it was Nula's turn. "I was the oldest of nine children. College wasn't really an option. I just wanted to provide for the family, so I started to work at the post office as a mail carrier. One day, on my route, I was walking between houses, and a kid, like a young goat kid, ran out into the street. The car didn't see her, so I ran out to protect her. The car should have hit me dead on and taken out the kid too, but my forcefield appeared, and we all walked away unscathed. The story about it blew up and went viral. Some local newspapers did stories, but because it was such a bizarre event, a lot of people thought it was a lie. I couldn't control the power and make it appear when I wanted. My siblings believed me and were excited about my powers, but my parents thought I was making it up for attention. When I couldn't prove them wrong, they asked me to leave home. Chee showed up a couple of days later, and I've been here ever since."

When Nula finished, she looked in Blank's direction, "Oh, my turn..." he was visibly uncomfortable and avoiding eye contact. "So, I was bullied a lot as a kid. Every day, the same kid would shove me into the lockers. One day, I went invisible, and I couldn't figure out how to go back to being visible again. I was like that for months. I tried talking to my parents, but when they couldn't see me, they freaked out. I just kind of existed without anyone knowing I was there. Master Chee found me, taught me in my invisible form, and helped me turn it off and then control my power.

Then, it was Master Chee's turn. "I think it's time we all go to bed."

Paul replied, "Absolutely not! Come on, Master Chee, how did you get here?"

The rat sighed, looked begrudgingly at his companions, and then gave in, "Oh, alright," he muttered before settling in to tell his story. "Unlike all of you, I grew up in a village on an island, much like this one, where superpowers were a part of our culture. While not everyone had powers, most did. Children were taught how to discover their power, teenagers learned how to control it, and adults used their powers to benefit the village. Those who didn't have powers were treated like everyone else. I had one student...a white alligator named Xavier. He believed for quite some time that he had no power. He grew angry and filled with hate towards those with powers..."

Master Chee's story was interrupted by Pip who began to scream uncontrollably. "AAAAAAHHHHHHHH!" Pip fell off his chair into the sand. He held his wings to his head and squirmed side to side repeatedly as if suffering an unimaginable amount of pain. Suddenly, he stopped. Pip's eyes shot open and locked with Paul's. "Your friends...they need help NOW!"

***

Five days earlier...

Brrrrriiiiinnnnnngggg Brrrrrrriiiiiinnnnnngggg

     Sam Hart was taking an afternoon nap on his couch. The sound of his phone ringing on the end table next to him abruptly ended the nap. With his eyes still closed, Sam stretched for the phone and answered, "Hello?"

     "Hey Sam, it's Boone. There was another break in at DragonCorp. I was hoping you could help…"

     "Another one? Is it that stupid Filthy Five or whatever they call themselves?"

     "No, they're still in custody…and this break in is a little different…I'll show you when you get here."

     Sam hurriedly got dressed, brushed his teeth, and headed to DragonCorp.

     When he got there, Boone was waiting for him at the entrance where Sam could immediately see the differences referenced by his friend. When the Garbage Gang had trespassed, they did so sneakily. Other than the tripped alarm, there weren't many signs of entry. This time, the trespassers were not so discreet. In fact, they weren't discreet at all. Rather than trying to pick the lock, the front door was ripped off its hinges and thrown several feet inside. The door frame had visible claw marks and chunks of rubble were left along the door's threshold.

     "Oh my!" Sam exclaimed. "I see what you mean, Boone. Did you already go inside?"

     "Yeah. Whoever it was knew their way around. Two more doors are ripped off. The security office where they kept the servers for the security cameras…those are all smashed. Then, they went into some kind of equipment storage room. Other than the missing door, not much was disturbed. I would presume they were looking for one particular thing…"

     "What kind of equipment?"

"Looks like a bunch of gizmos and gadgets," Boone chuckled. "I could push some buttons and try to figure out what they do if you want."

"Ha!" the lion laughed. "I don't suppose you have any idea what that *one particular thing* could be do you?"

"Not a clue. Maybe we could get that hyena friend of yours down here or escort Dr. Pigg, and maybe he could figure out what they took."

"Careful, you're assuming the swine isn't in on it! This beast could be working for Talon and/or Pigg. Bringing him down here to look around could play right into their hands."

"Good point. So, what do you think we should...." Boone's walkie-talkie interrupted the conversation.

Calling all officers. We have a situation downtown. All officers that are available, please report to 6th and Broadway immediately. The Garbage Gang is back.

Boone reattached the walkie-talkie to his belt. "I gotta go. You wanna come with?"

"I'm going to stay here and look around if that's okay with you, deputy."

"Alright, be careful." Boone left DragonCorp and headed downtown.

Sam turned and headed toward the forementioned technology equipment room. Just as Boone had reported, the door had been ripped off the hinges, and giant claw marks were left around the frame. Suddenly, Sam heard a sound coming from the room. The lion crept closer to the door. When he looked inside, he saw a figure behind some shelves. He clutched his cane, ready to use it as a club if necessary. Sam crept slowly forward to get a better look, but he didn't notice the bubble wrap in his path on the floor. He stepped on it, and the wrap let out a *pop-pop-pop.* The intruder heard this and fled further into the room. Sam followed. It wasn't a large room, but the shelves made a snake-like path to the back wall. The lion followed the path, and at the end was a closet door. Sam grabbed the handle, opened the door, and was surprised when he saw a familiar face, "What are *you* doing here? What is tha..."

SWOOSH

A freezing cold blast was shot at Sam. His cane clanged on the floor as the lion was frozen solid.

***

The next morning, a teenage hyena sat at a kitchen table eating her cereal while watching cartoons.

DING DONG

"Just a minute," the girl hollered in the direction of the door. The hyena reached down to her side, disengaged the brake on her wheelchair and made her way to the door. She unlocked the deadbolt, twisted the handle and when she saw her visitor, she greeted him with an excited "Uncle Henry!"

"Harley!" Henry the hyena replied as he went in for a hug. "My favorite niece! How are ya, kiddo?"

As they embraced, Harley smiled and rolled her eyes "I'm your *only* niece, Uncle Henry."

"Huh!" he joked "I guess I never realized that. Is Grandma here?"

"No, she had to go to work early."

"Well, that stinks." Henry looked at the television. "Um, aren't you a little old for cartoons?"

Harley blushed, "I was just flipping through channels..."

"Hey, isn't this *Mean Mr. Mustard*? Your dad and I used to watch this with you when you were little..."

"So, what's up?" Harley changed the subject.

"Oh, right." Henry reached into his pocket and pulled out a small vial filled with white capsules inside. "I picked up your next round of medicine for you."

"Uncle Henry! That stuff is expensive! How did you afford it? You're not..."

"You don't need to worry about where the money comes from, but if it makes you feel better, no, I'm not doing anything I'm not supposed to be doing."

Harley crossed her arms and shot a scowl at her uncle.

"Seriously, I have a legitimate job now, and some friends helped out too."

The young hyena girl's scowl disappeared and was replaced with an excited expression "SUPER PENGUIN?" she asked.

"I cannot confirm nor deny...but hey, the other reason I'm here. You dad has visiting hours today. Do you want to go with me to see him?"

"Yes! It's been weeks!"

"Alright! Go get ready. I'll hang out here." Henry took a few steps to the family room couch, sat down, grabbed the TV remote and changed the channel to a local station. There was a special report interrupting the usual morning show. The reporter stood outside of the prison where Henry's brother, Hank, was currently residing. "Just days ago, Eagle City Penitentiary experienced its first break in attempt in nearly 60 years, and now the prison is under attack again. The assailant appeared to have a plan and a unique weapon as he or she froze the inmates in some sort of permafrost. The only inmates that were attacked were former employees of DragonCorp. High profile members of the disgraced company were not excluded as Ulysses Talon also fell victim to the attack. Just days after being stripped of his "General" rank in our nation's military, Talon is now completely incapacitated and stuck in a block of ice. Doctors and other medical staff were called in and confirmed that all of those frozen are still very much alive and are in critical, yet stable, condition. Another interesting tidbit: oddly enough, there was *one* past DragonCorp employee who was *not* frozen."

Henry whispered to himself as he waited for the reveal, "Please be Hank. Please be Hank."

"Dr. Herbert Pigg. There's been no information yet as to *why* Dr. Pigg was excluded from the attacker's plan..."

Henry's eyes left the screen, and that's when he saw his niece. With her eyes welling up and tears beginning to stream down her face, Harley sat motionless as she began to cry. Henry stood up, rushed to his niece, and embraced her in a hug. "It's okay Harley. Your dad is going to be okay..."

KNOCK KNOCK KNOCK

The two hyenas looked at each other, confused. "Are you expecting anyone?" Henry asked his niece. She shook her head no. Henry tiptoed to the door and peaked through the peephole. The hyena let out a sigh of relief as he turned to his niece. "Don't worry, it's a friend." Henry turned back to the door, unlatched the deadbolt, and turned the knob.

"Hey Annie, it's good to see…"

The bear raised her arm and aimed a wrist-worn device at Henry.

SWOOSH

The hyena was frozen solid. Harley screamed at the sight of her uncle as Annie aimed her weapon at the girl.

SWOOSH

***

One day later, Police Chief Yu walked into her office to find a stack of manilla folders in her inbox. Each one contained a different case. The reports were similar. All of them had been called in within the last 24 hours, and all of them involved finding someone frozen in permafrost. The victims fell into two categories: former DragonCorp employees and police officers. As she sat down, Deputy Boone entered her office.

"Good morning, Chief," the dog said to the sheep. "You doing okay?"

"To be honest, Boone, no…no I'm not doing okay. We've got a goon on the loose freezing a third of our force and taking out DragonCorp employees while the company is going through its own investigation. If Talon wasn't frozen, we'd be interrogating him right now!"

Boone grabbed a small stack of the folders and asked the chief, "May I?"

Yu nodded.

Boone flipped to the front page of each folder and looked at just the names of the police officer victims. His tail started to wag. "Hey, Chief…did you notice the pattern with our officers?"

"What pattern?"

Boone kept looking through the folders to confirm his suspicions. "Each officer that was frozen was under investigation in the

DragonCorp bribes, so whoever is doing this, it looks like their motive is revenge…"

Yu stood from her chair and started rummaging through the folders Boone had reviewed. "Oh my gosh! You're right! This is huge! Great job, Detective!"

Boone's tail continued to wag. "Thanks! I'll go through the rest to make sure that it's not just a coincidence…also…I wanted to ask, has anyone heard from Sam? It's been a couple days…"

Yu's rejuvenated excitement dissipated. "You haven't heard?"

"Heard what?"

"I sent an officer to retrace your steps at DragonCorp…they found Sam…he was frozen."

Boone couldn't speak. He stared at Chief Yu for a moment, then the floor and finally the ceiling as he fought back tears. After a few moments composing himself, Boone broke the silence. "We need Super Penguin back."

"We've got no way to get ahold of him!"

"Okay, then we need Tundra…she's new to the hero stuff, but she's been around long enough that she can be an extra pair of eyes out there. Let me give her a call." The dog dialed the phone. It didn't ring and went straight to voicemail. "Ugh, I'm going to go out and see if I can find her. Is there anything you need from me before I go, Chief?"

"No, I'm headed down to the prison in a bit to interview Dr. Pigg."

"Is he still the prime suspect?"

"I think he's our *only* suspect right now. According to the guards, he's been a model citizen. Ever since the Garbage Gang break in, they say he's acted like a completely different person. We've been watching him all day and night, and he hasn't done much of anything. He cooperated with the interrogators, but they said his story was insane. I'm hoping I can get more out of him or at least get something that makes sense!"

"This is nuts! Okay, I'm headed out!"

"Be careful, Boone."

***

The portal appeared in the penguin's bedroom. Paul stepped through, followed by Nula and then Blank. Finally, Master Chee stepped through as Pip flew above. Nula looked around the room. She saw Paul's unmade bed and a pile of dirty clothes in the corner of the room. She grimaced, "Master Chee, why did you transport us into the room of a teenager?"

Paul clapped back, "Hey! Easy with that! I wasn't exactly expecting company!"

Pip peered out the window, "It's still light out?"

Blank answered, "Yeah, Pip. We just went back a few time zones when we went through that portal!"

"Woah!"

Master Chee interrupted the two conversations "Perhaps, we should make our way into another room to discuss our course of action?"

Paul agreed and led the way out the bedroom door and into his living room. They each found a place to sit. Master Chee and Nula sat on the couch, Blank took the matching recliner, and Pip perched on top of the floor lamp between the others. Once his guests were seated, Paul grabbed a chair from the kitchen and dragged it into the meeting place.

Master Chee spoke first, "Pip, now that you've had some time to collect your thoughts and emotions, please tell us what you saw."

"Okay..." he looked at Paul. "Just so you know, I've never had a vision like this. I'm not even sure if it means anything...but I saw your friends. The polar bear, she...she was locked in some kind of cage...and your lion friend, the police dog, and the hyena. All of them are alive, but they are stuck. They can't move...your enemy...the Komodo dragon...he's stuck too...he's not with them, but he's stuck in the same kind of way."

Paul, searching for understanding, asked Pip, "How do you know it's them and not some other polar bear or lizard?"

The bird replied, "I...I don't know...I just saw them, and I felt their connection to you. It's hard to explain. I'm sorry." The bird put his head down, embarrassed and upset with himself. "I'm still learning about my powers, too. That's all I know."

Paul replied, "Pip, there's nothing to be sorry about, dude! You're doing the best you can. That's all any of us ever expect."

Pip smiled. "Okay, let me close my eyes. Maybe I can see something else." The canary closed his eyes while the rest of the group watched. "Hmm...nothing yet...wait...okay...I... I see...I see a pig! He's also in a cage...but this one looks like it has metal bars. The one your bear friend was in...it didn't look like this..."

The penguin's eyes narrowed. "Dr. Pigg...I had a feeling he was behind this... Master Chee, can you take me to him?"

Nula chimed in, "You know where he is?"

"He should still be at the prison. Let's start there!"

Nula replied, "Sounds good. Before we go, are you showing up to this as 'Paul' or 'Super Penguin'?"

The penguin chuckled, "Good point! Let me get dressed first." Paul went back into his room and closed the door behind him. He walked to his dresser and went to his closet. Hidden in the very back were his suit and cape.

Once he was dressed, Super Penguin picked up the wooden bō staff he received on the island before opening the bedroom door and reuniting with the others.

Master Chee created a portal, but before they walked in, Paul had a concern. "Master Chee, where does the other end of this portal lead?"

"Just outside of Dr. Pigg's prison cell."

"That's what I was afraid of...they just had a break in a few days ago...so they probably aren't in the mood to be surprised by a magical portal. Let's start on the outside and get permission to go in."

Master Chee nodded. He waved his right paw counterclockwise, and the first portal disappeared. He waved his hand again clockwise, and a new portal appeared. Super Penguin stepped through, and the rest of the group followed. The new portal's exit was inconveniently placed in the back seat of a car- a police car to be more precise. The police car was currently being used by Chief Yu. The ewe had parked and was moments away from stepping out when Super Penguin's band of travelers suddenly appeared in the back seat.

"AH! WHAT THE HECK?!" Yu exclaimed. As soon as she did, she recognized a friendly face. "Super Penguin? What are you doing in my car?"

"It's a long story...like a *really* long story, but we're here to see Dr. Pigg. I think he is up to something...not exactly sure *what* he's up to, though."

"Well, isn't that convenient? That's why I'm here too... also on a hunch..." Yu replied.

Nula interjected, "Can we talk about this outside of the car? It's a little cramped back here."

"Yes, yes, of course," Yu answered as she got out of her seat, exited the car, and opened up the back door on the driver's side. Super Penguin's group filed out one by one and formed a circle.

Nula resumed the conversation, "So, what's the plan?"

Yu replied, "The warden's policy is only two visitors at a time, so I can take Super Penguin in, but that's it."

Master Chee spoke up, "Then we will wait out here until you return."

Super Penguin nodded. "I probably can't take my bō in there. Will one of you hang onto it for me while I'm in there?" Blank stepped forward and took the staff from the penguin. Chief Yu and Super Penguin made their way for the door, but after a few steps he realized he had more contraband on him, and he darted back towards his friend. "I probably can't have these in there either! Oops!" He pulled out his small collection of smoke bombs, this time handing his gear to Nula. "Okay, *now* I think I'm ready!"

Super Penguin and Chief Yu made their way to the pedestrian entrance. They met the guard, a panda bear, at the front gate and were approved to speak with the prisoner. They passed through the metal detectors with no issues and were escorted to Dr. Pigg's cell by another guard, a very strong rhinoceros. Dr. Pigg had been moved to a more secure location since the break in. Along the way, they passed through multiple checkpoints with bigger and stronger guards watching each post. First, a team of chimpanzees guarded the outer layer, then a pair of gorillas at the next checkpoint, then two more rhinos at the next stop, before they finally reached Dr. Pigg's cell, which had two elephant guards dedicated just to him. Each guard pulled a remote control from their pockets. The remotes weren't small per se, but they looked tiny when held by elephants. The guards simultaneously pushed a button on each of their remotes. In unison, they then lifted the remotes to their left eyes as a small, red light emitted from the remote and scanned their retinas. After this, several locks unlatched, and the door popped open. The guard on the right finished opening the door while the left guard had his gun unholstered and prepared to fire if Dr. Pigg tried anything. Finally, the right elephant addressed Yu and Super Penguin. "Take as much time as you need, but be careful. He's been babbling about all sorts of weird stuff. He's cray cray." Super Penguin and Chief Yu stepped in. One guard followed and closed the door behind them. It latched shut.

Dr. Pigg was laying on his bed, facing away from the door. The guard shouted, "Wake up, pig. You've got some guests." Dr. Pigg rolled over and glanced at his visitors. When he saw *who* the visitors were, he sprang to his feet.

"Ss...Ss...Super Penguin..." he nervously stammered and then gulped. "And you're the chief of police...wh..wh..what can I...how can I help you?"

Chief Yu replied, "Why don't you tell us what's going on Dr. Pigg." She stepped towards him. "Every scientist and grunt that ever worked for DragonCorp is frozen solid...except for you. Can you tell us *why* that is?"

"Y..yes, I can, but I'm not sure you will believe me."

Super Penguin replied, "It's been a pretty weird week for me. I'm willing to entertain just about any crazy story."

"Okay..." Dr. Pigg responded nervously. He wiped the sweat from his forehead and continued. "When I first started working at DragonCorp, I was quite nervous. I didn't know what I was getting myself into. The pay was very good, and they had been leaders in the field of technology for decades, but when I first met with General Talon, I quickly realized I had gotten myself into quite a predicament. I was given an ultimatum to work for him. Help him complete the robot project or face certain death. I was completely caught off guard. I didn't want to harm the city, but I also didn't want to die, so I started snooping around. One thing led to another, and I found some notes on a project that DragonCorp had been working on. This particular project was simply titled 'Experiment B' and had been an attempt at time travel."

"Time travel?" Super Penguin interrupted, "They tried to send someone back in time?"

"Not exactly," Pigg answered. "Rather than *sending* someone back in time, Talon's scientists attempted to transport someone's *soul* from present day to their body in the past. Essentially, today's mind would control yesterday's body. While they didn't succeed in their original mission, it seemed they still had quite the scientific breakthrough. They weren't able to transport the soul to the past, of course; the time travel paradoxes alone would cause countless issues...sorry, I'm getting off track. While they couldn't send the soul to the past, they *did* manage to separate the test subject's soul from his body."

"What? That's crazy? Who was the test subject?"

"He was a gorilla named 'Beau Nanas'."

Now, Yu interrupted, "The gorilla at the prison..."

"Yes. He had committed some pretty heinous crimes and was sentenced to life in prison. Talon made a deal with the warden to use him in the experiment."

Yu spoke up again, "Did Beau agree to it too?"

"He wasn't given the choice. It gets weirder too. When the scientists attempted the experiment, Beau's soul detached from his body, but it didn't *leave* his body. It wasn't until he touched one of the scientists that his soul transferred into her body, and he took control. Then, he used the new host to touch his own body, and his soul went back. When Talon found out that the time travel wouldn't work, he canned the experiment; however, one of the scientists, a penguin actually, wanted to know more about Beau's new ability. Talon agreed that Beau could be taken off site. The scientist put him in a secured apartment. It wasn't a very big building, three floors, and he had one of the floors to himself. It was converted into a holding cell- windows didn't open and doors locked from the outside. The scientist's family moved into the same building. Then, as luck would have it, the apartment complex caught fire. The scientist and the family died. Ironically, the Chief of Police lived there too. He... also died. Beau was pretty banged up but was found by a rescue team and brought back to the prison. I read all this in the file. I grew curious, so I went down to the prison to talk to Beau during visitor's hours. I was so stupid. As soon as I got there, Beau offered to shake hands, and I obliged. His gorilla body went limp, and my body was in his control. I was aware of everything he did with my body. I had to watch all of it. Trying to hurt you, Super Penguin, and Henry Cackle...I'm so sorry. I was under the gorilla's control until he used me to break back in...then, I woke up in this cell."

Yu replied, "Well, that does sound pretty crazy, but we need to consider all stories right now...Super Penguin what do you...hey...Super Penguin, are you okay?"
Super Penguin's face was expressionless as he ignored Yu's question. "You said this gorilla was in a fire with the former Chief of Police and a penguin family..."

Before Dr. Pigg could respond, a portal appeared in the room. Super Penguin's bō shot into the room and hit the wall. It rolled to Super Penguin's feet. The penguin picked up his weapon and looked back at the portal. Master Chee leapt through the opening and somersaulted on the ground. The rat stood, rapidly turned, and closed the portal behind him as quickly as he could. A blast of cold air filled the room as the portal closed.

"Well, that was close!" Super Penguin stated. "What the heck's going on?"

"Your bear friend is here. She's here for Dr. Pigg. We must leave, now. All of us."

"I don't understand," Super Penguin grimaced as if he was staring at a difficult puzzle. "What does Annie want with Dr. Pigg? And I thought Pip said she was locked up in a cage." The penguin looked at Dr. Pigg, and the puzzle began to piece itself together. "Oh, no!"

Yu inquired, "What is it?"

The penguin turned to the prisoner. "Dr. Pigg, when Beau transported into someone else, did he have to touch them, or if he was touched by someone else, could he transfer that way too?"

"Any physical contact with Beau would create a bridge into their body. Once he's in control of another person's body, he can't jump to someone else. He'd have to go back to his body and create a new bridge."

"Annie fought Beau during the breakout...she punched him...she's...oh my gosh. That's why she's been acting so weird!"

A voice was heard on the other side of the door as one of the elephant guards yelled, "Hey! What are you doing here?"

Super Penguin's focus shifted to the matter at hand. "We need to get out of here now! Master Chee, where are the others?"

"Frozen. We will discuss this later, but we need to leave now!" With that, Master Chee opened another portal. "Follow me!" Master Chee went through, then Dr. Pigg, then the elephant guard, then Super Penguin, and finally Chief Yu.

The party appeared on the roof of the prison. Master Chee closed the portal behind him. "As long as we all keep our voices down, we should be safe up here."

Super Penguin replied to the rat in a panic, "What are we going to do about Pip, Nula and Blank?"

"There's not much we can do for them at the moment. We need to pause, plan, and then execute, but we must do it in that order. If we challenge Tundra right now, we will surely lose."

"Okay," Super Penguin looked at his peers, "any ideas?"

Dr. Pigg replied first, "You said the others are frozen? Is this the DragonCorp tech?"

"Yes," Yu answered. "Is this something you built?"

"N-no...but I'm familiar with how it works. I could build something to counteract it, given the right equipment. It would all be at DragonCorp..."

Super Penguin asked, "So if we get the parts, do you think you'll be able to unfreeze them?"

"Yes, I believe so."

Super Penguin clapped his flippers together. "Alright, Master Chee, portal us over there!"

Master Chee did not comply. Instead, he posed a question, "What good is unfreezing if the bear can still re-freeze them? We must solve the root of the problem and stop Mr. Nanas."
The group nodded and audibly agreed.

Dr. Pigg's face lit up as he had an epiphany. "This is just a hypothesis, but when the scientists performed the experiment, they had a special stone. They called it an *Enoch Crystal* and it's known to have some kind of special properties."

Master Chee smiled. "I'm quite familiar with those crystals, and as for the *special* property you are referring to, I believe the word is *magic*."

Super Penguin smiled. "Master Chee...were you just...sarcastic?"

The rat continued to smile. "A little bit. I learned that from you Mister Fr...I mean, Mr. Super Penguin." Super Penguin rolled his eyes at being called *Mr. Super Penguin.*

Master Chee continued, "There is a cave deep in the forests of an island nation called Koalastantinople. These crystals can be found there. The cave is protected by fierce warriors who have guarded these treasures for centuries."

Dr. Pigg jumped back into the conversation, "With those stones, I think I can duplicate the original experiment and modify it in a way to save your friend."

Super Penguin clapped his flippers together again. "Alright, sounds like a plan. Let's get to it! Master Chee, fire up the portal to Koalastantinople!"

The rat, once again, did not comply. "I cannot."

"What? Why not?"

"The village itself is protected by a magic. No portals or other modes of teleportation can be opened from the outside going in. I could use a portal to leave there but not to enter."

"Okay. Can you get us close?"

"Yes."

Super Penguin clapped his flippers together one more time. "Alright, then let's do that! Get us as close as you can and..."

But once again, Master Chee stopped things before they started. "I am not permitted to be there."

"Okay, seriously? What the heck?"

"We don't have time to get into the details, but my presence there would ruin the mission. I'll transport the three of you..."

Now, Chief Yu interrupted the conversation. "I can't leave Eagle City. Tundra is under control of a bad guy, and if Super Penguin is gone, I need to be here to protect the city."

Master Chee nodded. "That seems very wise. I'll also stay here and monitor Miss Tundra and Mr. Nanas."

Super Penguin replied, "So just me and Dr. Pigg? That's fine, I guess...can we leave now?"

Master Chee answered, "Well, actually..."

"OH, COME ON!" the penguin complained. Master Chee smirked, then Super Penguin laughed. "Another joke? What's gotten into you, Master Chee?"

The rat smiled, waved his hand, and a portal appeared. Super Penguin and Dr. Pigg stepped through, and the portal disappeared behind them.

***

At the other end of the portal, Super Penguin and Dr. Pigg arrived at the edge of a forest. Behind them was a sea of wild grasslands on a hilly plain. In front of them was a collection of trees, hundreds of feet tall, as far as they could see to their left and to their right. Master Chee's portal had conveniently placed the pig and the penguin at the starting point of a dirt trail that weaved through the forest.

Super Penguin quickly scanned the area. "I'm guessing it's this way," he said as he pointed at the path. With no reason to disagree with Super Penguin's guess, Dr. Pigg nodded in agreement, and the two began walking. The trail was long and winding but had no forks- only one way in and out. Dr. Pigg and Super Penguin walked side by side.

the trail was just wide enough for them to do so. They were silent for the first leg of the trail, but after a little while, Super Penguin broke the silence.

"Hey, Doctor Pigg?"

"Please, call me Herbert."

"Ok, Herbert...when you told us about that Beau Nanas guy...you mentioned a fire..."

The swine nodded as he listened intently.

"Who did you say was in that fire?"

"Well, there on the top floor was Beau's cell, and then below that was the Chief of Police at the time, Samuel Hunt, or Hart...something like that. And then, on the ground floor, was the scientist that was monitoring Beau and conducting more research on his condition."

"Do you know the scientist's name?"

"Well, yes. I believe the reports said 'Doctor Frost'."

Super Penguin stopped in his place and shouted, "You're wrong!"

"P-p-pardon me?"

"My parents were the penguins in that fire. My dad was a doctor...but he wasn't monitoring anyone! And he *certainly* wasn't working for DragonCorp!"

"You're...the doctor's son...I...I'm sorry...I didn't know!"

"TELL ME YOU'RE LYING! TELL ME YOU MADE IT UP!"

Super Penguin was fuming. He encroached on Dr. Pigg now inches from his face. Dr. Pigg submissively stepped back, but with each backwards stride, Super Penguin matched it.

The two had lost any and all awareness of their surroundings, so they didn't see the trap they were about to step into. A large ditch had been dug and then covered with sticks and leaves to trap the unobservant.

Dr. Pigg fell first and was immediately followed by Super Penguin who landed on top of his companion. Super Penguin rolled off of the swine, and the two stood, dusted themselves off and looked up to see the fifteen-foot hole they had fallen into. Climbing out was a hopeless endeavor as the steep walls were barren of any footholds or handles. As they looked up, koala bear heads began to appear, peering over the chasm to look at their prisoners. First one, then a couple more, and then there were so many heads. A ring of koala bear faces had formed around the entire circle.

Suddenly, a penguin head appeared and smiled. The penguin's voice, familiar only to Super Penguin, called out, "Paul?"
In disbelief, he replied, "Mom?"

***

The mother penguin slid into the hole on her tailfeathers and embraced her son. "Oh, Paul! It's so good to see you again!"

"I... I'm so happy," Super Penguin replied, as a tear streamed down his beak. "I'm so confused though. Why are you here? Is Dad here with you?"

"We should...um... let's get out of this hole and I'll explain everything." The mother penguin had almost forgotten that she and her son were accompanied by Dr. Pigg. She broke off the hug, but with her left flipper still positioned around her son's back asked, "So, who's your friend, Paul?"

"Mom, this is Dr. Pigg. We...um... are here on a mission to save Eagle City...and I just realized I have *a lot* to catch you up on, too!"

The mother penguin extended her flipper. "Nice to meet you. I'm Piper Frost."

Dr. Pigg engaged in the pleasantry excitedly. "It's a pleasure to meet you, Dr. Frost. My name is Dr. Herbert Pigg."

"Please, call me 'Piper'," she replied. Then, she looked up the walls of the ditch and spoke to the koalas above, "Ooga ooga, oog oog ooga." One koala stepped away as the others continued to spectate. A rope appeared and unraveled from the one absent bear's place. The mother penguin motioned for Dr. Pigg to climb up first, then Super Penguin, and finally Piper herself. She looked at the koalas, let out one loud, "OOG," and the koalas dispersed back into the trees. "They're a curious bunch but good listeners! Follow me. I'll take you to the chief."

"Okay, and maybe let me know how the heck you're still alive!"

"Yes, of course, and maybe you can tell me about that outfit you're wearing!" Piper laughed and began walking down the trail. Super Penguin caught up to her and walked on her right. Dr. Pigg trailed a few steps behind.

"I'm serious, Mom! Five minutes ago, I thought you were dead, and now you're next to me. I went to your funeral! How are you here?"

"I'm sorry. It's just not an easy story to tell..." Piper's voice became shaky.

"Would it be easier if I asked you questions? Like an interview?"

"I think that might help. We can try that."

"Okay, is Dad here with you?"

Piper sniffled and wiped her eye, "No."

"Did he make it out of the fire?"

She paused, sniffling longer and louder as tears now streamed down her face, "No."

"Did Dad work for DragonCorp?"

Quicker than the last two answers, "No!"

Super Penguin looked back at Dr. Pigg, "See. I told you my dad wouldn't have worked for them!"

Piper continued, "I did."

Super Penguin stopped walking and stood, almost frozen. After a moment, he started, "What?"

Piper had turned and faced her son, but she looked at his feet, ashamed "I...I did. I worked for DragonCorp." Just off the edge of the trail, a tree had fallen years prior. The mother penguin sat down on it. "Let's sit, and I'll explain."

Super Penguin complied and sat next to his mom.

"When you went off to college...I struggled. Financially, we were fine, but I'd been a science teacher for so long, and my role as your mom had changed...call it a mid-life crisis, or needing a change of scenery, or whatever, but I was struggling. There was a job posting for a biologist at DragonCorp, and so I applied. I didn't think I would get it. When I went in for the interview, I was, by far, the oldest applicant, and I had spent the last 20 years working in a school...but I stayed and did the interview, and, lo and behold, I got the job. I didn't know what the project was, and I had to sign several non-disclosure agreements before my first day. I wasn't even allowed to tell your you or your dad that I was working there. Your dad knew I had a new job and that I applied there, but I *technically* never told him that I started working at DragonCorp. After all the legal paperwork had processed, I was assigned to a time travel project. There were about ten of us working on the experiment. Our lead scientist aimed to send a test subject's mind, memory, and soul from present day into their past body. To do that, I had two jobs. The first was the physical care of our test subject, a gorilla named Beau. My second job was using my geology background to aid in the experiment in any way. We had no leads. Everyone was making hypotheses and seeing them through. In my research, I learned of these crystals, Enoch Crystals, and found they were on an island- *this island*. I made a trip here and met with the chief, and they allowed me to try to earn a crystal through something they call *Temple Challenge.* I was successful and took a crystal home. We used it in an experiment on Beau, and while he wasn't transported anywhere, his soul was removed from his body. While removing heart monitors, I touched his hand, and his soul transported into my body. He took over for a moment before he touched his own body and was transported back out. I reported my findings, and we tried a couple of other experiments, but the time travel attempts never worked. Talon scrapped the program and fired most of the scientists. He wanted to know more about Beau's power, but he didn't want him on sight. Beau was moved to an apartment building that was modified to be a containment chamber for him. I had to convince your dad to move into the same building so Beau could be monitored at all times. It wasn't easy, especially since I wasn't allowed to tell your dad about the experiment. My team was just me and a couple of security guards who helped keep Beau from getting out of line. We ran some different tests but struggled with making any headway on the experiment. Beau wasn't the most cooperative test subject either. He frequently resisted, and the rhinos would have to subdue him. When the experiment didn't produce any findings, Talon's secretary fired me over the phone. He told me the project was over. I asked what we were going to do about Beau, but he had hung up before I got an answer. I went down and talked to Beau and told him what happened. That's when I found out he was a convict and the *trade* that had happened between Talon and the prison. My mind was racing a thousand miles an hour. I went back to our apartment until your dad came home. When your dad got home, I told him I needed to go for a walk. I went down the street to get dinner, and as I was walking back... *sniffle*... I saw that the apartment had collapsed and was on fire. I don't know what happened, but I assume DragonCorp was behind it. I panicked and ran. I didn't know where else to go, so I came here and have been living with this koala tribe ever since."

Super Penguin was dumbfounded. "Why didn't you tell me?"

"I was afraid. Would the attackers stick around to make sure I was dead? Would they connect me to you, and would that put you in harm's way? I know it was wrong to abandon you like that, but I thought it was the best way to keep you safe. And I knew you had Annie to watch out for you."

"Well, now Annie needs *our* help. Your *experiment* survived the fire too! He's in control of Annie as he goes on a revenge tour getting back at everyone who ever wronged him."

"Oh, dear!" Piper exclaimed. "Well, then what are you doing here?"

Dr. Pigg spoke up, "I studied your experiments. I believe I can alter a few things and break Annie free."

Piper stood up, "Okay then! Follow me!"

"Mom, wait!" Super Penguin got up and gave his mom a hug. "I'm glad you're okay."

***

The trio continued down the trail and arrived at the entrance to the koala village. A large wall made of old trees bound together surrounded the village and formed a square compound. At each corner stood a tall wooden turret with a pair of koalas inside, each wielding a bow with a quiver of arrows on his or her back. In the middle of the front wall was a draw bridge that dropped over a ravine. As they approached, the bridge was lowered, and a koala walked toward them. He was dressed more formally than the other koalas they had seen. This one wore a long red robe that dragged behind him and a crown made of woven leaves. Super Penguin approached, bowed, and spoke to whom he presumed was the tribe's leader or at the very least a person of importance.

"Hi. My. Name. Is. Super. Penguin. I. Come. In. Peace."

The koala turned to Piper and pointed at Super Penguin. "Is there something wrong with this guy? Why's he talking like that? And what's with the cape?"

Piper laughed, "Sorry. He *just* met the Ooga brothers and probably thought all of the koalas here talked like they do!" The two shared a laugh. "Super Penguin and Dr. Pigg, this is Mike."

"Mike?" Super Penguin questioned. "Not Ooga Booga Boo? Or even Chief Mike? Or Prince Mike? Just...Mike?"

The koala smirked, "Yep, just regular old 'Mike'. What can I do for you?"

Piper interjected, "Mike, this is my son, Paul. He's a superhero back home." Then, she pointed towards her other companion. "And this is Dr. Pigg. They are in need of an Enoch Crystal to save their home."

"Are you a superhero too?" Mike asked pointing to Dr. Pigg, but Mike continued asking more questions before the swine could respond to the first one. "How come he's in a cape and you're wearing that?"

Dr. Pigg looked at the bright orange prisoner's jumpsuit he was wearing.

"Well, you see..."

"Yes!" Super Penguin interrupted, "He's a superhero, too."

The koala chief replied, "Oh okay....and what is a supe...you know what, never mind. Any friend of Piper's is a friend of mine. I'd be happy to help, but, Piper, you know the rules. I can't let you back into the trials. These two will have to go alone, and they only get the one shot. They've not been trained. Do they even know what they are walking into?"

"Well..."

"You didn't tell them?" Mike directed his attention to Super Penguin and Dr. Pigg. "Guys, I'm going to level with you. The Enoch Temple trial isn't something to be taken lightly. It'll test you mentally, emotionally, and physically. Some have even died attempting it."

Super Penguin didn't flinch. "Annie needs my help...and...so does the rest of the city. I probably should have swapped the order of those, sorry. What I'm trying to say is I'm willing to do what it takes!"

"I like your spunk, kid." Mike glanced over at Piper. "Chip off the ol' block." He looked back to the younger penguin and pig. "There are a total of nine rooms set up in a three-by-three grid. You'll start in the southwest corner and make your way to the final room. If you pass a trial, you'll move closer to the goal. If you fail a trial, you'll move closer to one of the exits, and if you don't make it out...well, then I have to send in the Ooga Brothers to clean up the mess."

Super Penguin ignored that last part. "So, Mom, you've done this before. Can't you just tell me what's in there and how to beat it?"

"I wish I could, but that's not how the trial works."

"What do you mean?"

"There are nine rooms, and at most one person can see five of the obstacles, but there are over 100 different possibilities as they rotate in different challenges. The odds of you having one of the same challenges that I did is quite small. The odds of having all of the same challenges I had, that's nearly impossible."

"Oh, I see. Are Dr. Pigg and I allowed to go in together?"

"Yes, any number of people can go in, but you each only get one chance. You have to decide if you'd rather have two chances separately or one chance together."

"Hmm," Super Penguin thought aloud. "What do you think, Doc?"

"I've always believed two heads are better than one, and I don't think I'd be able to pass this on my own, but perhaps I could help you a time or two."

"One hundred percent agree." The penguin looked back at Mike and Piper. "Alright, we are going to do the trials together."

The koala chief replied, "Sounds good! Let's get started! Oh, wait, before we go, you won't be able to take any gadgets or gizmos in there with you, so please leave those...you can keep the cape on though."

Super Penguin relinquished his bō from his person and handed it to Piper. Dr. Pigg searched his orange prison jumpsuit before realizing the silliness of what he was doing "Haha!" he giggled, "It would have been a bit problematic if I *did* have something wouldn't it?" The penguins chuckled while the koala was confused, but he smiled as if he knew what they were talking about, since he was still under the impression that the pig's outfit was worn by superheroes, not inmates.

"Alright, let's head to the trials!"

Piper hugged her son, "Go get'em, Paul!"

Mike led Super Penguin and Dr. Pigg out of the hut and down another trail. After a five-minute jaunt, they arrived at the temple. It was an imposing structure, built of sandstone, with ancient drawings on the side. The characters in the drawings were mostly koalas, but Super Penguin noticed a picture that looked eerily familiar. A pig and a penguin...that appeared to be wearing a cape. "What's that?"

"Ancient prophecy," the koala replied. "Don't worry though, there's all kinds of penguins that have come through here."

"Really?"

"At least two," he said with a smirk. "You're the first one with a cape though."

Dr Pigg inquired, "What's the prophecy?"

"Nice try, doctor. First rule of prophecies: If a guy shows up that looks like a prophetic temple drawing, and you tell him what the prophecy is, it's not going to come true if you tell him about it."

"Fair enough," Dr. Pigg replied.

They continued walking up to an entry way with a large stone door and a stone button positioned similarly to a doorbell on most homes. Mike pushed the button, and the door sank into the ground. "This is the entrance to the temple. Your first challenge begins as soon as you walk into this room. Good luck, guys."

***

Super Penguin and Dr. Pigg stepped into the first room. Two steps in, the door rose from its crevice and slammed shut.

There were two more doors in this room- one to their right and one directly across from them. Torches on the walls lit the room, and in the center sat a stone table with various items spread around on top of it. There were tools such as a mallet and chisel and various fruits carved out of stone, and, in the center of the table, a large stone bowl. In front of the bowl sat a stone push button and a stone tablet with a message carved into it. The tablet read, "Satisfy the bowl by filling it with the answer to the riddle below. When you are ready for the bowl to be judged, press the button." Super Penguin read the riddle aloud, "Take away my first letter, and I still sound the same. Take away my last letter, I still sound the same. Even take away my middle letter, and I will still sound the same."

Dr. Pigg immediately hit the button.

Super Penguin shouted, "Wait!" but he could not stop the swine in time. The door to their right opened. A carving on the floor, like a doormat, was revealed. It read "PASS."
Super Penguin turned to his comrade with a look of shock and excitement. "How'd you do that? What was the answer?"

"When I was a child, I'd frequently complete riddles with my father. I remembered this one from the many we'd read. The word was *empty*. If you take away the 'e', *mpty* still sounds like *empty*. Then, if you take away the 'y', it's still *mpt*, which still sounds like *empty*. And last but not least, if you take away the 'p,' it's *M-T*."

"Wow! Nice job, Doc!" Super Penguin offered up a fist bump, and Dr. Pigg reciprocated. "Alright, onto room two!"

The penguin and the pig walked through the doorway, and after a couple of steps in, the door closed behind them. Once again, there were two more doors- one to their left, and one straight ahead. They scanned the room and noticed another stone table, but instead of being in the center, it was tucked in the corner to their right. Super Penguin approached it with Dr. Pigg a step behind. A bow and three arrows lay there with another stone button and a stone tablet with directions. "A Test of Skill: Push the button and a target will appear. Hit the target with an arrow within fifteen seconds to pass."

Dr. Pigg looked to Super Penguin. "This is absolutely not something I will be any good at. I suggest you take this one!"

"I've never shot a bow and arrow before, but I'll give it my best shot!"

Super Penguin grabbed the bow and readied an arrow while Dr. Pigg was ready to hit the button at his partner's command. "Now!"

Dr. Pigg pressed the button. A wooden, circular target sprung down from the ceiling about twenty feet from where Super Penguin stood. The penguin released the first arrow but missed to the left. He grabbed the next arrow and drew the bow back, but just before he released, he fumbled the arrow. Super Penguin reset with the arrow in place, pulled back the bowstring and released. He over corrected, and this arrow narrowly missed to the right. He grabbed the third arrow, pulled back and ERRRRRR. The alarm sounded. Time was up. Super Penguin released the arrow anyway. Bullseye. A door opened to their left. Like the previous room, it revealed a message on the ground; however, this stone floor mat read "FAIL."

"Not to worry," Dr. Pigg said as he patted Super Penguin on the back. "It's one to one. We have more trials to go! We'll get them on the next one!"

The two trial-goers walked through the next doorway to a room with another table in the middle and one stone door to the left and one to the right. Super Penguin and Dr. Pigg made their way to the table where they found another stone bowl on a platform with instructions etched into a stone tablet. "Fill this bowl with exactly four liters of water to advance. There is no time limit, but you only get one attempt." Along the wall, directly behind the table, sat a small fountain. Super Penguin and Dr. Pigg investigated the fountain and found two bottles, one labeled "5 Liters" and the other, slightly smaller bottle labeled "3 Liters."
Super Penguin took the five-liter bottle, filled it most of the way up, and said, "That looks like about four liters. What do you think?"

"Whoever wrote this underlined the word 'exactly', so I have a feeling eyeballing it isn't going to work."

"Yeah, you're probably right. Let's figure this out."

The penguin and the pig experimented: filling bottles, emptying them, and repeating the process several times in a row. Then, something clicked in Super Penguin's brain. He filled the five-liter bottle with water and grabbed the empty three-liter bottle. "Hold this for a second," he directed Dr. Pigg. Dr. Pigg obliged. Super Penguin then carefully poured water into the empty three-liter bottle. "Ok, so now I've got two liters in here," Super Penguin gestured at his bottle. "Now, dump yours out." Dr. Pigg obliged again. "Next, I'm going to pour these two liters into your bottle." Super Penguin did as he said, and before he explained anything further, he refilled the five-liter bottle. "Okay, now we've got five liters in mine and two in yours. If I fill yours up, that'll take just one of my five liters, and this bottle will have four liters in it!"

"You're right! Great work!"

Super Penguin carefully poured the one liter from his bottle into Dr. Pigg's and then poured the remaining four liters into the bowl. The bowl lowered its base and made a loud *CLICK*. Moments later, a stone door rose and another "PASS" doormat was revealed.

"Alright!" Super Penguin exclaimed. "That's two! One more to go!"

The two animals made their way through the doorway but quickly realized that this door was unlike the previous ones they had walked through. Instead of another room, they had entered a hallway just a tad wider than the door itself. After a few steps, they noticed the floor began to slope downward and curved to the right in a large half circle. Like the rooms, torches lit the hallway along the way, and the width of the room gradually got larger the farther down they went. When they reached the end of the hallway, they found two doors with a message carved into the wall between the two exits. The message read, "Beware: The Final Test is very dangerous. The door on the left is your chance to resign and return to the village unscathed. The door on the right will take you to your final challenge."

Super Penguin stepped toward the door on the right. "Wait!" Dr. Pigg exclaimed. "I... I'm not sure I can go through with this!"

"Huh?" Super Penguin remarked. "I'm so confused... we've come this far."

"I... I'm scared. I'm not as brave as you are, Super Penguin."

The penguin stepped back towards his partner and put his wing on the pig's shoulder. "Hey Doc, I don't know if this will make you feel any better, but I'm scared too."

"You don't seem scared. In fact, you seem exceptionally brave right now. You were going to walk in there without thinking twice about going through this other door."

"You know, for a really brilliant doctor, you're not very smart."

"Now, I'm confused," said the pig.

"I'm very afraid of whatever is in this next room, but I'm choosing to be brave. Being brave doesn't mean I'm not afraid. I'm afraid, like, *all* the time! I just choose to face what's making me afraid instead of running away from it."

"Oh," Dr. Pigg seemed to have an epiphany. "So, being brave is a choice...I'd never thought of it like that before."

"Doc, I'm going to be *very* real with you right now. I am absolutely terrified of what's in this next room, but I wouldn't have gotten this far without your help, and I'm a little less terrified of whatever is in there with you by my side."

Dr. Pigg was speechless for a moment. Then, he smiled and simply said, "Thanks, Super Penguin."

"Alright, well let's get in there and try not to die!"

***

Super Penguin and Dr. Pigg stepped through the doorway on the right. The room was dimly lit with the only light emitted from a few torches on the walls. This room was nearly quadruple the size of their previous rooms. They looked around for instruction but only found a large mass of crystals in the center of the room on a mound of stone. The crystals were a blueish-green color, a shade darker than turquoise, and gave off a dim glow.

Super Penguin asked, "You think that's the Enoch Crystal?"

"I think so...not much of a trial though. It could be a trap, so let's be careful."

They slowly tiptoed atop the dirt floor on their way to the crystals and then stepped up onto the big rock.

Dr. Pigg looked it over. "This looks like what we want, but how do we remove it?" The swine took his eyes off the crystal and scanned the room looking for a pickaxe or any other tool. There was nothing in sight.

Super Penguin wrapped his flippers around one of the rocks and pulled "Ugh!" he grunted as he tugged. "Well, that didn't work!"

Suddenly, the ground began to tremble, and the stone surface began to rise. The surface tilted, and the duo slid down the side of the rock and back onto the ground. Super Penguin landed on his feet while Dr. Pigg tumbled into the dirt. He laid on the ground for only a moment and was quickly back on his feet. Dr. Pigg dusted off what he could while he looked at the phenomenon. The rock started to move as if it was slowly turning around. As it turned, it first reveled two large appendages that looked like arms and two stone legs. A few steps later, it revealed its face. Its eyes were two large, black spots, and its mouth was a crevice with sharp rocks that acted as its teeth.

"Wh..what is that?" Dr. Pigg exclaimed.

The rock creature let out a loud, "ROAR!" and slammed its arms into the dirt. BAM! A shockwave shook the room, and the duo struggled to stay on their feet. As they wobbled, the monster pulled a large rock out of the dirt. It raised the small boulder behind its head and chucked it at the heroes.

Super Penguin dove left.

Dr. Pigg dove right.

The projectile avoided them both.

The monster let out an angrier and louder, "ROAR!" and charged at Super Penguin. As it ran, it wound up its arm to throw a punch with its large, boulder appendage.
Super Penguin ducked.

The rock monster's fist bashed into the wall. The room shook, and pieces of rock fell from the ceiling.

Dr. Pigg yelled out, "I don't think we're going to be able to wear it out! We need to subdue it or destroy it!"

Super Penguin nodded and replied, "You got any ideas for slowing it down? I'm leaning towards figuring out how to destroy it!"

The rock monster turned towards Super Penguin, roared again, and charged. It drew its arm back again to punch, so Super Penguin ducked under again, but this time the rock monster kicked. The force of the kick sent Super Penguin soaring across the room and into the stone wall. He hit it with a THUD and slid to the ground. "That one hurt," the penguin said as he rose to his feet.

The rock monster placed the end of its rock arms onto its rock belly and let out an "AH AH AH!"

Super Penguin asked Dr. Pigg, "Is it laughing?"

"I think so!"

"Alright, that's it!" Super Penguin began to glow a purple hue. "Hey, Rocks-for-brains! I'm not finished!" The purple glow got brighter and brighter. Then, it became such a light purple it was nearly white.

The rock monster's laugh stopped. It turned back towards Super Penguin and, once again, began to charge.

Super Penguin charged back at it. When he was close enough, rather than ducking again, Super Penguin wound his flipper back and threw a punch of his own. The purple energy moved and concentrated to the end of his fist.

Their fists collided.

Super Penguin blacked out for a moment. When he came to, small, fist-sized pieces of rock were strewn around the room. Most of the crystals had shattered too, but Dr. Pigg found one that was still intact. He grabbed it and then said to Super Penguin, "That was incredible. Are you alright?"

"Yeah," the penguin replied still trying to get his wits about him. "Is that the crystal?"

Dr. Pigg nodded. "It is."

The final door opened, and Mike, along with five more koalas, ran inside. While the others began searching the floor for an unknown something, Mike shouted at Super Penguin and Dr. Pigg, "What on Earth happened in here?"

Super Penguin, with a dash of pride in his voice said, "We took care of your monster! He put up quite a fight!"

"You FOUGHT him?"

"Well, yeah. What were we *supposed* to do?"

"The final test was supposed to teach you about non-violent conflict resolution. You were *supposed* to be able to figure out that you couldn't beat Enoch in a fight! *If* you stopped to talk to him, he'd ask what you wanted. *If* you had asked him nicely, he would have just given you one of the crystals off of his back."

"Oh...well he tried to fight us first!"

Dr. Pigg chimed in, "Well, we did attempt to pull the crystal out of his back first."

Super Penguin's face began to turn red from embarrassment.

One of the koalas in the corner yelled out, "Mike, I found him over here!" The koala was holding a spherical stone about the size of a lunchbox. The stone had eyes and a mouth, just like the monster they had seen moments before. Mike rushed over to it. "Oh, Enoch, my little buddy, I'm glad you're okay."

Super Penguin whispered to Dr. Pigg, "I am so confused right now. Is that his pet?"

Dr. Pigg shrugged.

Mike turned back toward the penguin and the pig. "Take your crystal and get out of here. Kurt is just outside and can teleport you back to your homeland." Then, the koala went back to nurturing his pet rock.

The duo did not hesitate. They made their way out of the room and down a trail back into the village. As they walked, Super Penguin tucked the crystal into a pocket located on the inside of his cape. Piper stood at the end of the trail with their belongings and two koalas. "I heard you two made quite the mess in there!"

"You heard about that already?" Super Penguin replied to his mother while strapping his wooden bō staff on his back.

"Don't worry. Enoch has been through *much* worse."

"Really?"

"Um...well, no, probably not. I don't recall any stories of him being blown up before...but the *important* thing is he's okay. It'll take him some time to grow back up to that size and make more crystals, but other than that he's fine."

Super Penguin looked relieved, "Well, I'm glad he's alright, and most importantly we got the crystal! Now, let's get back to Eagle City!" Super Penguin hugged his mom and said, "I'm going to miss you, Mom."

"I could go with you!"

"What? No! It's way too dangerous! If Beau sees you, who knows what he'll do!"

"I'm, at least, partially responsible for this mess. I should help clean it up!"

Dr. Pigg added, "Dr. Frost, I could use your help with building the machine."

"It's decided then!" Piper cheered.

"Alright," Super Penguin surrendered. "I can see I'm not going to win, so I'm not going to stop you, but that doesn't mean I don't think it's a bad idea!"

Piper collected her things, and the group found the koala named "Kurt" who had teleportation powers that could return the group. "Okay, everybody hold hands, and someone tell me where we are going." the koala requested.

Piper answered first, "Eagle City!"

***

A cloud of smoke appeared in the middle of Paul's kitchen with a loud BAMF!
Once it dissipated, Super Penguin, Dr. Pigg, Piper and Kurt the koala appeared from behind the smoke.

"Whose kitchen is this?" Piper asked with a look of disgust on her face. "It stinks in here! Those dishes look like they've been there for days, maybe even weeks! And the floors..."

"This is my place, Mom. I've been kinda busy."

"Oh," she paused, "well if you'd just tidy up a bit..."

"MOM!"

"Sorry."

Dr. Pigg chuckled, "We should probably get going."

"Wait...what's the plan, again?" asked Super Penguin.

"Well, I guess we never fleshed that out, did we? So, for starters, we need to get to DragonCorp. From there, we have two projects. First, Dr. Frost and I need to reverse engineer her old experiment to find a way to extract Beau from Annie. Second, we need to find something that will melt the permafrost weapon so we can thaw out those that Beau has frozen."

The pig and two penguins looked at the koala.

"Ugh, fine, but then I'm going home," Kurt sighed. They all held hands and BAMF!

The group was teleported to the entrance of DragonCorp. The yellow police ribbon was still in place and the building still vacant.

BAMF!

True to his word, the koala had disappeared.

"Well, that was rude!" Dr. Pigg exclaimed.

"Yeah, but not surprising. He's the 'office jerk' back at the village," replied Piper.

Super Penguin chimed in, "I don't remember seeing any offices!"

His mother rolled her eyes and ignored her son's smart aleck comment. "My machine is long gone, but I should be able to get the parts I'll need in the warehouse. Dr. Pigg and I will head there. Paul, you should head to weapons storage. If there's not another one of those permafrost guns, I'd bet the blueprints and notes are there. If we know how it's made, I'm confident we can reverse the effect. Go find that, and we'll meet back here."

Super Penguin left the group and headed for the weapons storage area of DragonCorp. The campus was large but well labeled. Above each intersection hung a sign that had names of each department with an arrow pointing towards the path to get there. He followed the arrows until he found the door to weapons storage, still open. The penguin cautiously walked through the doorway and began to scan the room. He noticed a familiar looking cane on the floor a few steps into the room and started talking to himself. "I'd bet anything this is Sam's." Super Penguin clinched his flippers into fists, and they began to glow purple, but the color soon dissipated. He picked up the cane and scanned the room. Horizontal icicles had formed days earlier in a subtle outline of where Sam once stood. "Sam was definitely in here looking for something. I must be on the right track." The penguin kept searching the room and found a box of gauntlets. He grabbed the top one in the box. The gizmo looked mostly finished. It had a sleek, silver exterior with a red button labeled "IGNITE" in white lettering where a watch would normally sit on one's wrist. At one end, there was a nozzle-like part where it seemed something would be expelled. Super Penguin attached the device to his flipper, with the nozzle pointing away from him, and pushed the red button. A jet of flames shot out three feet from the device. The penguin quickly tapped the button again, and the flames got bigger and shot out farther. He hit the button a third and fourth time, and, once again, the flames grew bigger and bigger. The emergency sprinkler system kicked on, preventing the fire from spreading, but the steady stream of flames continued to flow from the device. Super Penguin quickly but carefully removed the gauntlet, set it on the ground and smashed it with Sam's cane. After a few strong swings, it was reduced to pieces and no longer shot out fire. "Let's try another one."

The penguin went back to the box of gadgets and found a similarly shaped device, but it seemed to be missing its outer shell. Instead of the sleek, silver finish, its outermost layer was a collection of wires running longways across the gizmo with a circuit board at one end. This one also had a *yellow* button labeled "IGNITE" in black. Super Penguin assumed something would come out, like the previous gadget, but he didn't see any indication as to *where* it would come out. He pushed the button and ZAP!

The water from the sprinklers above mixed with the electric weapon and created a cloud of electricity around the device. It backfired in a small electrical explosion. Super Penguin's body was flung into the wall behind him with a loud THUNK. His feathers, usually matted down, were now standing straight up all over his body, with the occasional spark jumping from feather to feather. He sat for a moment, taking in what had just happened and then moaned, "What the heck?! Who leaves something like that laying around?" Super Penguin slowly stood back up and smoothed his feathers. He said to himself, "In hindsight, pushing random buttons in a *weapons closet* probably *wasn't* the best idea in the world. But luckily nobody saw that! Maybe I should change gears and look for some blueprints." Super Penguin began to scour the room, and, on a shelf a few feet away from the gadgets, laid a pile of large, blue, rolled up papers. "This has gotta be it!" he said aloud to himself. He unrolled one and looked at it confused. He rotated it ninety degrees, then another ninety, and then back to its original orientation. He opened another and completed the same ritual. "I'm clearly not smart enough to understand *any* of this." The penguin scooped up all the rolled-up schematics and tucked them under his wing. "I'll let the brainiacs figure it out!"

Super Penguin left the room and went back the way he came until he arrived at the spot where the group had separated. "That's weird. I figured they would have been back before me." The penguin looked outside the front window in case they were outside. "Nobody out there, just Annie's van." It clicked. "ANNIE'S VAN!" Super Penguin sprinted down the hallways, frantically looking for the signs guiding the way. The penguin ran so fast that he nearly toppled over each time he made a turn. As he got closer to his destination, he could hear the familiar voice of his best friend. Super Penguin reached the doors of the warehouse. He slowly opened them and peaked inside. The polar bear was facing away from him, and just beyond the bear, he could see Dr. Pigg and his mom.

Dr. Pigg looked scared, a look Super Penguin had seen several times since their team up. Piper, however, looked prepared to fight despite the obvious size and strength disadvantages she clearly had.

Super Penguin crept closer and could now hear Beau's lecture.

"You! You did this to me! And then you tried to have me killed!"

Piper stood her ground. "I had no idea what Talon was planning! I promise! They tried to kill me too!"

"Liar!" the possessed bear growled. "You just *happened* to be away when they staged the attack? You'll pay for what you've done!" Beau aimed the permafrost blaster at Piper. "In fact, why don't we settle up right now!"

"Hey! Bozo!" Super Penguin came out from behind the door. "Leave my mom alone!"

Beau turned around and roared at Super Penguin. "You just couldn't stay out of this, could you? The goody-two shoes penguin who didn't have anything to do with any of this keeps sticking his beak where it doesn't belong! Just like that rat and that sheep that were following me around, I'm gonna have to freeze you too!" The gorilla-controlled polar bear aimed his blaster at Super Penguin.

WHACK!

With his back to Piper and Dr. Pigg, Beau missed their ambush. Piper swung a pipe at the bear's head, and Dr. Pigg swung another at the blaster. It began to spark. Beau roared angrily. He tried to fire the ice blaster, but nothing happened. He swiped at Dr. Pigg, and the swine soared into a wall, rendering him unconscious. Next, Beau swiped at Piper, and she suffered the same fate as the pig. Beau ripped off his ice blaster and tossed it to the ground. Super Penguin began to glow purple. "YOU SHOULD HAVE LEFT MY MOM ALONE!" he screamed as he charged. While running, he removed his staff from his back and swung it at the bear. The energy transferred from the hero to the staff and then to the bear, sending his foe flying through the air and into the wall.

Beau began to laugh as he got to his feet. "Silly bird, did you forget your friend is my host? I can't feel any of this. You're only hurting her!"

Super Penguin's face sank. How could he defeat a foe that he could not physically harm? The bear was now charging at him, but the penguin dove out of the way. Once he missed, Beau grabbed the same pipe that he was previously struck with and flung it at Super Penguin. The bird dove under it, narrowly avoiding the weapon, but it was only a distraction. As soon as Super Penguin could get back on his feet, a large bear foot struck him in the chest, sending him soaring through the air and into the wall. Super Penguin heard something break. It wasn't the sound of one of his bones, but rather something fragile like a glass dish. "Oh, no," he thought to himself, "the crystal!" The hero reached into his cape pocket and found fragments of what was once a whole piece of the Enoch Crystal. "Think, think, think!" Super Penguin said to himself. "I can't hurt this guy without hurting Annie, the two geniuses who know anything about this rock are unconscious, and now the dang thing is broken into multiple pieces! Think, think, think."

Then, as if Master Chee was speaking to him, he heard his voice. "Fly like a penguin. Find your own way!"

An idea sprung to his mind. "This is either going to be genius or absolutely the stupidest thing I've ever done." Super Penguin clutched the shattered pieces of the crystal in his right flipper, charged at the bear, ignited his purple energy, wound back to punch and...

***

The warehouse was gone. Super Penguin found himself in a black space with no windows, furniture, or anything else. There was no floor, walls, ceiling, or sky. It wasn't dark; however, it was as if he was illuminated. He could see himself as if it was the middle of the day, but he could see nothing else in front of him. He turned, and there on the ground he saw Annie, chained to a chair with her mouth gagged. Next to her, also on the ground, was a gorilla. It was the same gorilla he had seen at the prison days before, again wearing an orange prison jump suit. Super Penguin went over to aid Annie by first removing the gag and then working on the chains.

"Boy, am I glad to see you!" Annie exclaimed. "Confused as all get out with *how* you got here but excited none the less!"

"Where exactly is *here*?"

"You're in my mind, Supes!"

"I was afraid you were going to say something like that!"

"Pretty trippy, right?" Annie was now unchained. "Like, you're not *actually* here, but your mind is *in* my mind. If that makes any sense."

"It's actually getting weirder and more confusing the more we talk about it."

"No kidding!" Annie retorted. "Imagine being me. One minute, I'm in complete control of my body, and the next minute I'm having this weird out-of-body experience but *inside* my body."

The gorilla began to move.

"Uh oh," Super Penguin noticed Beau coming to. "Any ideas of what to do with him?"

"I suppose we'll fight him," Annie said matter-of-factly.

"Will my powers work here?"

"Powers?"

"Oh, right, I never told you."

"Just kidding, I saw them when you took down the Garbage Gang. I mean it wasn't me in control of me, but I still saw it."

"Still weird, and you didn't answer my question."

"You're not *you* right now, Supes. You're just your mind. I think you can do just about anything you can imagine."

"Hmm, I wonder if..." Super Penguin began to glow purple. "Alright! No staff though. I wonder if..." and suddenly his wooden staff appeared in his flippers.

"Alright, Annie. Let's do this!" Super Penguin looked back at his friend, who was now in her complete superhero uniform.

"Do I have to keep telling you? It's *Tundra*!" She cracked her knuckles.

The gorilla got to his feet with a confused look on his face. "How did *you* get in here?"

Super Penguin replied, "That's not important. What *is* important is it's time for you to leave!"

The penguin and bear charged towards the gorilla. They each threw a punch. Tundra went high, Super Penguin went low, but Beau Nanas dodged both attempts. He seemed to move in a blur, faster than what was physically possible, because it was.

Super Penguin and Tundra kept punching, and Beau kept dodging.

Beau mocked them. "Ha! This is mind over matter! I've been doing this longer than either of you! You cannot defeat me!" He leapt back what seemed like fifty yards.

Super Penguin turned to Tundra. "We have to fly like penguins!"

Confused, she inquired, "What are you talking about?"

"Long story, but the short version is, we have to do this *our* way. Let's think differently!"

"Okay, I think I get what you're talking about...so you're going to fly around?"

"Well... actually, that's a great idea!" and with no effort at all, Super Penguin began to hover. He flapped his wings a couple of times and was now face to face with Tundra. "What are you going to do?"

"We're in my mind, right? Watch this!" The floor, or lack thereof, began to shake, as if there was an earthquake.

"What the heck!" Beau yelled. "How did you do that?"

"You're on my turf! My rules!"

"Stop that!" the gorilla yelled.

Super Penguin soared towards Beau. When he got close, he twisted his body and delivered a kick to the gorilla's torso. Beau fell to the ground, which was still shaking, and he struggled to stand. When he got close to getting his balance and standing upright, Super Penguin would deliver another soaring kick!

After a couple of kicks, Beau leapt into the air and floated there. He too was flying now.

"I've got another idea!" Annie stopped the tremors and created a large cage around Beau. Captured, he fell to the ground. The gorilla then turned himself into a goo and slithered between the bars! Once he was outside, he retook his original shape.

"You'll have to do better than that!" Beau mocked.

The heroes and Beau went back and forth. Annie would create something, and Beau would counter with his own creation.

Super Penguin looked at Tundra and put his flippers out, motioning for her to stop trying things. "What do you want, Beau?"

"Revenge! I want DragonCorp destroyed! I want everyone to pay for what they did to me!"

"Those things have already happened! General Talon is in prison. DragonCorp is done-zo."

"That's not good enough! They took something from me. They took my freedom!"

"I saw your rap-sheet Beau. You gave that up when you committed those heinous crimes!"

"Ha! Is that what they told you? That I was some criminal? That I *deserved* it? The only crime I *ever* committed before I became DragonCorp's little test subject was being homeless. Talon saw me as less than because I slept on the street near his headquarters. He saw me as worthless and expendable. I traded my body for meals and some shelter. The contract he wrote up was supposed to provide for me for the rest of my life. He told his scientists I was a convict. Somewhere in their twisted sense of morality, he thought they'd be against experimenting on a homeless gorilla but have no problem running tests on a *bad guy*. And then the cherry on top. *As soon as* his project flops, the *moment* it goes sideways, what does he do? He hires his goons to off me!"

Super Penguin set down his staff, walked towards the gorilla, and hugged him. The gorilla resisted for a moment, but eventually he gave in.

"I'm sorry, Beau." The gorilla didn't respond. He just wept.

"This isn't the right way to handle it though. I've got an idea to make things right, but I need you to surrender. No more fighting."

Beau released from the hug, wiped a tear from his face, and nodded in agreement.

"Tundra, can you check on Dr. Pigg and my mom?"

"Yeah, they are up now."

"Do you mind if I..."

"Yeah, go ahead."

Outside of Tundra's mind, Super Penguin spoke through his friend's body. "Hey, this is Super Penguin. Beau has agreed to surrender, but we need your help getting out of here."

Dr. Pigg replied first, "How do we know it's actually you in there, Super Penguin?"

Piper answered for him, "It's him. A mother always knows her son's voice, even if it's coming out through a polar bear. How can we help, son?"

***

Over the next few days, the group followed Super Penguin's plan.

First, Dr. Pigg and Piper used the Enoch fragments and rebuilt Piper's machine. Once that was back together, they helped return Super Penguin to his body.

Next, Beau identified the location of all of the frozen bodies. Once Master Chee was unfrozen, he created a portal for Super Penguin and Tundra to retrieve Beau's body. Beau transferred back to his body with no further incident. Super Penguin, Tundra and Beau went back into the portal together. In Sam's secret base, a meeting was held. In attendance were Super Penguin, Tundra, Dr. Pigg, Piper, Master Chee, Sam, Chief Yu, and Beau.

Super Penguin led the meeting. "First off, I want to thank all of you for being here. There are a lot of moving parts and decisions we need to make. I think the right thing is to decide this together. But first, Chief Yu, did you find Beau's records?"

"I did. There are some pretty serious crimes listed, but when I dug into those, it was pretty obvious they were fabricated. The officers who wrote the reports were all Talon's goons, and there's no history of these crimes actually happening."

Sam chimed in, "But he *did* commit some crimes while hijacking Annie and Dr. Pigg's bodies."

"That's also true," Super Penguin acknowledged.

Master Chee added, "But would he have committed any of those crimes if he hadn't been the victim of Talon's undiscovered crimes?"

Yu replied, "Also a good point."

Piper spoke up, "I have an idea." The group turned to her. "What if he came back with me to Koalastantinople? We'd make him work to earn his keep, and it would also be a fresh start."

Beau replied, "That's awfully generous, but I don't deserve that."

Piper responded, "You didn't deserve anything that happened to you when I worked for DragonCorp. This is the least I can do."

Chief Yu added, "As the representative of law enforcement, I think that sounds like a fair option. Tundra and Dr. Pigg, you two were victims in this. Are you okay with this arrangement?"

"Absolutely," replied Tundra.

"Me too," answered Dr. Pigg.

Chief Yu turned to Beau, "Are you okay with all of this?"

The gorilla smiled, "Yes, ma'am."

"Anyone opposed?"

Everyone shook their heads side to side slowly.

"Alright, then I think our work here is done! Thanks everyone!" Chief Yu left the hideout first.

Piper bid farewell to everyone else. Then, she spoke to her son.

"I'm so proud of you, Paul."

"Thanks, Mom. I'm a little surprised you aren't staying."

"I know. I wish I could, but this is what I need to do."

"It's okay, Mom. You're doing the right thing. And I can still come and visit! Well...hopefully I'm allowed back on the island...will you put in a good word for me to Mike?"

She chuckled, "My son will *always* be allowed on the island!" Then, Piper hugged her son and turned to the gorilla. "You ready to go, Beau?"

The gorilla replied with a smile, "Yes!"

Master Chee created a portal, and one at a time, Piper then Beau stepped through it returning to their island. Then, Master Chee turned to Super Penguin. "Excellent work, Mr. Frost. Top marks! I look forward to continuing your training!" He bowed to his student, then waved to the rest, created his own portal, and returned to his island.

Tundra turned and spoke to Sam and Super Penguin, while Dr. Pigg observed. "I...um...I need to say something, but I don't exactly know how to say it." She wiped a tear from her eye. "I think I need a fresh start too. I did a lot of bad stuff, and I know *I* didn't *actually* do anything, but that's not how the average citizen sees it. They see me as the polar bear who froze a bunch of people and got away with it because of some crazy story. I really want to do the hero thing, and I don't want this whole situation to muck that up. But I don't want you to be mad at me for leaving you either."

"Annie," Super Penguin replied, "you're my best friend in the world. If you think this is best for you, then you have my full support."

"I agree with the kid" Sam added.

"Thanks, guys. *sniffle* I don't have anything figured out yet, but there's a crime reporter opening in Newt Jersey, and they have a pretty high crime rate in that area. Maybe I can do some good there."

"Can I go with you?" Dr. Pigg asked. "All the things you said about what happened to you happened to me too, except you just froze a bunch of people. While my body was being controlled, I invaded a city with an army of robots and then broke into a prison with the same robot army. There's also a couple of looming attempted murder charges towards you and Mr. Cackle. My point is, I could use a fresh start too, and it would be nice to know someone in my new place. Maybe we could even do some good together!"

Annie smiled, "Sounds good to me, Doc!"

"Oh, thank you so much!"

Super Penguin asked, "How soon are you leaving?"

"I'm thinking next week."

"Alright, well, let's make sure we get a couple of trips to Tina's in before you go!"

"Sounds like a plan, Supes!"

Acknowledgments

This book (and its predecessor) would NOT be possible without the support of so many people. It may be my name on the front of the book, but without the following people, this book would not exist. Time for some shout outs!

Mom and Dad! Thank you for always supporting my dreams, even when they seem wild and crazy. Even when you disagree with the what and the how, you've always had my back, and I appreciate that so much!

To my editor and friend, Cindy. Thank you for the hours and hours you spend reading through the ugliest versions of the *Super Penguin* stories to help improve them! I can only imagine the sloppy mess these books would be without you!

To my best bud, Gardner. You are the perfect wingman for this adventure. You've found a way to be the Robin *and* the Alfred to my Batman. You're always by my side for the events and conventions and always coming up with ideas and suggestions to make Super Penguin better. When I need a fellow nerd to bounce ideas off of, you offer up the feedback I need. You're the best best-friend a guy could ask for, and I'm so thankful for you, dude!

To the SP fans (or anyone who has ever said anything nice to me about *Super Penguin*). Your kindness and support motivate me. I think all creators suffer from Imposter Syndrome and self-doubt from time to time, but with every kind word or gesture, the negative voices in my head get a little bit quieter.

To my little guy, Parker. You inspire me every day and fuel me to keep going. I want to show you by example that no matter how crazy your dreams may be, they are worth chasing.

And last, but not least, to my wife, Halley. Thank you for believing in me before I believed in myself. Even when my book-related adventures put more pressure on you at home, you encourage me to keep pursuing my dream.   I love you so much.

Tina's Diner was closed. It had been for well over an hour, but the lights were still on, and three figures were still inside. Tina stood behind the counter cleaning the last of the day's dishes. In the furthest booth from the door sat the cheetah, Michael Myles, and an alligator wearing a black turtleneck and a matching miller cap. While his outfit was rather plain, his appearance was quite stunning. Rather than the typical dark green, this gator's scaly body was white, and his eyes were a sharp blue.

Their conversation was interrupted with a knock on the glass of the front door.

Myles rose from his seat and approached the door nonchalantly. He unlatched the deadbolt and greeted the hooded figure.

"Lyla."

The tiger pulled back her hood. "Myles."

He pushed the door open for her, and she followed him inside. They walked back to the leucistic alligator. Lyla sat in the booth first and slid inside, then Myles sat next to her.

The alligator extended his hand. "Nice to meet you, Lyla. Thanks for taking the job."

"Nice to meet you too, mister...."

"Just call me Xavier."

"Well, Xavier. Thanks for breaking me out of that prison! I'm excited to hear what your plans are for taking out Super Penguin."

The gator smiled showing all of his sharp white teeth. "Let's get started."